ACCLAIM

"Nobility, courage, self-sacrifice…these are the themes explored in Brigitte Cromey's precious, deep-hearted novella. We live in dark times, and desperately need stories like these to help us find the light of hope. This is a tale after my own heart, and I will read it again and again in the days to come."

—AMBER KIRKPATRICK, author of *Until the Rising*

"Such an amazing page-turner filled with absolutely everything I love—political intrigue, princess/bodyguard romance, and swoony moments that keep drawing me back to read them again and again. This story is sure to please fans of Tara Grayce and K.M. Shea."

—BRYN SHUTT, author of *Illuminare*

"Guardian's Oath is a delicious blend of adventure, magic, and heart. Brigitte Cromey crafted a lovely story perfect for fans of childhood friends-to-more, forbidden love, and royal romance. Readers will find themselves rooting for the characters as they evade danger within their own borders, as well as their feelings for one another."

—CRYSTAL D. GRANT, author of *Shadowcast*

GUARDIAN'S OATH

BRIGITTE CROMEY

YARROW LEAF PRESS

Guardian's Oath

Copyright © 2025 Brigitte Cromey.

All rights reserved. No part of this publication may be reproduced, distributed, or transmitted in any form or by any means, including photocopying, recording, or other electronic or mechanical methods, without the prior written permission of the publisher, except in the case of brief quotations embodied in critical reviews and certain other noncommercial uses permitted by copyright law.

NO AI TRAINING: Without any limitation on the author or Yarrow Leaf Press's exclusive copyright rights, any use of this publication to train generative artificial intelligence is expressly prohibited.

This is a work of fiction. Names, characters, places, and incidents are products of the author's imagination or are used fictitiously.

Cover design by Luisa Galstyan

This edition published by Yarrow Leaf Press.
First published in *Crowns: A Heartbooks Anthology* by Quill & Flame Publishers

Paperback ISBN: 979-8-9850208-5-4
Ebook ISBN: 979-8-9850208-6-1

www.wordsinmyblood.com

To the ones waiting for someone to see them.
You're never as invisible as you think.

GUARDIAN'S OATH

1

BEFORE

THE PRINCESS'S FIRST UNDERSTANDING of the matter came after a playfellow's innocent question.

"Why don't you have any cousins?"

Her nurse, upon the repetition of the question, cupped her charge's face in her soft hand and stared into the princess's eyes for a long moment.

"Come with me, Tali." Her other hand stayed around the girl's as they went to the study, where she pointed to an embroidered wall hanging beside the fireplace. "You see?" Her wrinkled finger caressed the stitching, tracing down the names of Talianna's forebears until she came to a long, unbroken line—a tree with no branches, ending in a single name.

Talianna Victoria Marie. Princess of the house of Emrys.

"You, little one, are the only daughter of an only son." The nurse knelt beside Talianna and hugged her shoulders. "The only child of your line. And one day, sweet"—she raised the child's hand to her lips, little realizing how well her charge was listening—"you'll be queen."

That night, after her nursemaid put her to bed, Talianna lay awake for hours, the burden of expectations and responsibility settling on her eight-year-old shoulders.

She finally whispered her promise into the darkness, the creaking trees beyond her windows the only witnesses to the vow. *If this is to be my life, I will study hard and listen well to become the queen they all expect me to be.*

"So do I swear."

TEN YEARS LATER, TALIANNA stood atop the dais on a darkened spring evening. By then, the lonely years had acquainted her with the particulars of the matter—with no siblings and a mother long bereft of strength, the weight of the crown would fall upon her head, and hers alone. It was a fact not lost on the enemies of the realm, and the last few years had seen increasing threats to her safety. On this night, a week after an assassination attempt had claimed the lives of both her history tutor and guard captain, the faces of the few advisors around the dais were drawn with worry.

The young man who now knelt before the king had been the subject of much discussion by the court, the ink of his appointment not even dry before the gossips began whispering.

A knight, recently reassigned from a border posting.

Second son of a baron—barely nobility at all.

Hardly worthy of the position, but not many would accept a role that equated to well-paid servitude and a constant threat of death.

Young. Too young, this "Gavin of Andel."

Once Talianna had heard the name, memory sketched in the remainder with painful clarity. She'd once known Gavin's laugh, green eyes, and companionable nature as well as she knew her own reflection, before duty and study had driven them both from childhood games. His hair had once been the color of sunlight, but the years had tarnished it to a dull blond, made darker by the shadows creeping through the edges of the hall as he swore his oath.

"I, Sir Gavin of Andel, do solemnly swear to guard the princess Talianna to the fullest of my ability. May the blows of those who seek to cause her harm fall upon my head. May her enemies be my enemies, her danger my danger, and her life my life." The knight raised his head to look her in the eye, and a flicker of a smile crossed his face before retreating behind solemnity. "This do I swear, until my king releases me from my oath or I perish in the fulfillment of my duty."

Talianna extended her hand for her new protector to kiss, the last words of his oath settling around them in the stillness of the hall.

Both of us are bound to our oaths of duty, me as surely as him. The dreams of childhood will have to stay where I left them.

2

MIDWINTER

WINTER WEATHER POUNDED AGAINST the windows of Talianna's sitting room as Gavin stood before the fire. A storm had been threatening them all week and had finally broken in fury on the eve of the midwinter festivities. Fine grains of snow sifted against the small-paned windows as the wind whistled down the chimney. Even with the cold outside, the room was bright and warm. The fire danced merrily against hardwood logs, its cheerful crackle mixing with the giggling coming from behind the door to Talianna's dressing room.

"Sir?" A spare man clad in crimson velvet approached the fireplace. A chamberlain, no doubt come to take him to task about the princess's lateness to the ballroom. "Sir, the High Steward begs me to inquire…"

"Yes, yes." Gavin straightened his dress clothes as he went to the door connecting Talianna's private rooms with the rest of the suite. Animated conversation could still be heard beyond, and he rapped hard on the polished wood. "Your Royal Highness? Your father's becoming irritated at you."

"He can wait," Talianna replied from behind the door, her words punctuated by an amused laugh. "I'm almost ready."

"I'm sorry." Gavin turned to the servant with an apologetic smile. "She has a mind of her own. It shouldn't be too much longer."

As the door closed behind the chamberlain, Gavin resumed his place in front of the hearth. Within a few minutes, the dressing room door clicked open, and Talianna appeared, trailed by a handful of maids and ladies-in-waiting. In the two and a half years since he'd assumed command of her personal guard, the bright eyes and rounded cheeks of his childhood friend had melted into the sophisticated lines of a young woman with dark hair and sharp wit. Her burgundy and gold skirts rustled as she walked to stand beside him, a gleam in her eye as she measured her height in high-heeled slippers against his.

Gavin smiled. He was still taller. "Your shoes won't avail you much," he said with a grin. There had been a time in their childhood when the girl, two years younger than him but propelled by genetics, had been taller than he was. He turned his foot so she could see. "I'm wearing boots."

"Ah well," she sighed. "I still had to check." She glanced at the door. "Is my father very upset?"

Gavin crossed his arms and raised an eyebrow. "No. Unless you count the *three* chamberlains he's sent to ask if you're ready to be announced yet."

"It would be unforgivably rude to keep them waiting any longer." She gave him a mischievous grin, deep brown eyes flashing against her glowing skin. "He must've noticed I was postponing my entrance as long as I could." Her voice dropped low enough for only those nearby to hear her. "Between us, I can't stand the Treluthian ambassador."

Gavin snorted as the rest of the girls tittered. With a sigh, Talianna crossed the room to where yet another chamberlain hovered anxiously. "Thank you for your patience. Will you tell the High Steward that I am on my way?"

The man bobbed a quick bow and scurried away as Talianna swept into the receiving room, trailed by her ladies-in-waiting. Gavin followed, keeping a few paces behind Talianna as they proceeded from her rooms in the direction of the public areas of the palace.

The corridors gleamed with holiday decorations, and the scent of pine and holly filled the air from the garlands lavishly decking the tops of floor-to-ceiling windows. The figures of the girls ahead of him were almost dwarfed by the height of the hallway, the bright colors of their gowns an excellent foil against the darkness of the winter storm outside.

From this vantage point, Gavin could see the exact moment that Talianna assumed her public personality. In the amount of time it took to pass from one corridor to another, her back straightened and she seemed to grow taller. The laughter in her voice changed, as if each note in her voice was being carefully tuned to perfection. He sighed, wishing he hadn't first noticed the change several years ago. The Talianna he knew of old was bubbly, warmhearted, and practically sparkled from within. The version of herself she always presented to the court was more subdued—shimmeringly beautiful, perfectly composed, gracious, imposing—the image of the perfect royal heiress.

No matter how often he witnessed it, the change never failed to sadden him.

The ladies-in-waiting stopped ahead of Gavin as they approached the gilded ballroom doors. They fluttered around and adjusted each other's appearances before the chamberlains ushered them inside. Talianna stood to one side, her face utterly composed. She reached up to adjust her gold and pearl tiara as the last of her ladies passed through the doors. "How do I look?"

Gavin smiled. She unfailingly asked this question before every state event. After two and a half years of being near her, he recognized it as her way of assuring herself that at least one person could still see the girl behind the public façade.

"You look terrible." He raised an eyebrow as he stepped into his usual position a few feet behind her. "I'm not even sure why anyone would bother coming to this dinner, knowing you'd be there to spoil it."

She laughed, the public persona settling over her features with a sigh as she stepped up to the double door. A wash of light and color filled Gavin's senses as the heralds pushed open both doors, gold and crystal shining from the walls and ceiling of the grand ballroom.

"Her Royal Highness, Princess Talianna." A hush spread over the ballroom as the crowd of lords, ladies, diplomats, and honored guests sank into low curtsies and bows, their formal attire making the assembly appear as rich and vibrant as the contents of a jewel box. Talianna swept across the threshold, acknowledging the crowd before regally crossing the floor to greet her father and the Treluthian ambassador.

Gavin frowned as he slipped through the doors, taking in the assembly with one keen-eyed sweep. The queen was not appearing tonight, it seemed. Although Her Majesty was much beloved by her people, her appearances in such formal settings as the Midwinter Ball were few and far between. Talianna had once confided in him that her mother's illness was progressing rapidly, to the dismay of those who knew her best. Whatever the manner of the queen's failing health, it meant Gavin's dealings with Talianna's parents were relegated mostly to her father—a strong man and good ruler, and one determined to see his line continue at all costs. *Though so far, not by pressuring his daughter to marry.*

Gavin shook the relieved thought from his mind. His feelings for Talianna had long since crossed the border from friendship to something deeper, but any slip would mean the end of their friendship *and* his role of guardian. The reminder prompted him to check the dagger at his side—its decorative hilt made it less sturdy than he would have liked, but it was nevertheless the only weapon *anyone* was allowed to carry into the ballroom.

A foolish idea, but at least it means no one's tripping over a sword they can barely use. Gavin eyed one of the courtiers as the man escorted a lady to her seat at one of the long tables surrounding the perimeter of the hall, stifling a smile at the fellow's pompous gait. *Better to leave the swords to those who can use them.*

He flicked his eyes toward the ballroom doors, where crimson-uniformed guardsmen could be seen beyond the threshold. Other members of Talianna's personal guard were interspersed among them, their dark blue uniforms less conspicuous but their gazes sharper as they surveyed the hall. He gave a small nod to himself, satisfied that—at the very least—reinforcements were close at hand, should they be needed.

As servants began appearing from the kitchen entrances to place dishes of lavish food on the tables, Gavin skirted the edge of the hall to take his place with his back to the wall a few yards from Talianna's chair. The other guardians—those of the king and foreign delegates—greeted him with stilted nods before returning to their examination of the crowd of revelers. Gavin settled into parade rest, allowing his mind to sink into the routine of scanning the crowd and observing the patterns of servants as they served the guests by rank. He could still feel the wind vibrating past the roof, an occasional gust making a howling sound as it swirled past the edge of the hall. Talianna glanced back at him, and he gave her a reassuring smile.

Don't worry. I'm here if you need me.

Talianna fidgeted in her chair as one of the servants placed a steaming dish of soup in front of her. She waited for her father to take his first bite before dipping her spoon into the creamy liquid. With her mother's growing frailty, she'd had to steadily take on more responsibilities in the years since Gavin had become her guard commander. By this time, it was second nature to slip in and out of the version of herself that everyone needed to see: strong and flawless, the very embodiment of hope in the future.

The storm could still be heard whistling beyond the roof of the hall, and she wished she could be enjoying this meal in her room with her friends. Even though she'd long resigned herself to the demands of public life, she couldn't deny the pleasure of quiet nights spent in good company.

"It's a beautiful evening," her father said as he leaned closer. On his other side, the Treluthian ambassador was deep in conversation with his companions; no doubt comparing the styles of their balls to the ones in his homeland. "Isn't it, my dear?"

Talianna didn't have to manufacture a smile for her father. "It's glorious. I always love seeing all the pretty dresses and jewels the ladies put on display for the evening."

"Some more than others," her father said, a hint of a chuckle running through his voice as he nodded in the direction of the lower tables.

She looked where he'd indicated and raised an eyebrow at the sight of several noblewomen's dresses: obviously expensive, but in colors and cut that made her think of the sordid tales whispered by those of her ladies with older brothers. "That is…" She searched her imagination for the appropriate word. "That is spectacular." One of the foreign delegates laughed on the king's other side, his voice somewhat louder than manners dictated, and she leaned closer to her father. "Though, this year things seem a bit—oh, I'm not certain. It's like everyone is trying too hard to make things bright and beautiful. It feels forced, I suppose."

Her father nodded almost imperceptibly. "Things are tense," he admitted in an undertone. "It was never in the plan for the emissaries to remain here over the winter holidays, but the storms along the coast—" He stopped talking as the servants arrived to collect their soup bowls and lay the next course before them. "Well, it wasn't something I had anticipated, but we must always be courteous to our neighbors. I only wish they weren't so perceptive; some of them are starting to ask questions about you. I suppose they must've heard rumors."

She set her fork down with a deep breath. "Rumors regarding?"

The king gave a quiet shake of his head. "Just the usual. Mostly wondering why I haven't announced my heir's betrothal yet, now that you're so close to coming of age. I won't lie to you and say that I'm not concerned myself, but—"

Talianna cast a glance at the tabletop, aware that her stiffening shoulders would spell the tension clearly for anyone who happened to be watching. It took true effort to raise her head and speak as lightly as if they were merely discussing idle gossip. "If you're concerned, you know that you have every right to make the decision on my behalf."

Even as the words emerged, she wished she could take them back. *Don't be foolish,* she chided herself. *The choice of a husband is the one thing this role allows you for yourself. Don't throw it away.*

"Tali," Her father set down his knife and squeezed her hand—a gesture tantamount to a full hug. "Don't worry. I'm not so anxious as to take your choice from you. It's a pressing matter, to be sure, but"—he withdrew his hand and sat back as the Treluthians at the other end of the table laughed again—"I'm certain whomever you select will be entirely worthy of both your hand *and* your responsibilities."

Talianna sighed, her appetite gone as her father turned his attention to their guests. It was this ongoing conversation that, with each iteration, made the weight of her impending marriage press further onto her shoulders.

Worthy. A word that, on the surface, meant the usual things—of good character, an acceptable rank, well-educated and better spoken. Over the years, it had taken on a meaning of its own; one that now felt as mythical as a dragon, and unfair as a fight against one.

It's your choice, but remember…

It's your choice, but make it count.

Without meaning to, she found herself turning her head to catch a glimpse of Gavin, his presence like a warm fire behind her. It was a habit she'd fallen into once she'd realized he was one of the few who saw through the persona she donned for each public event. Longing struck unexpectedly, and she had to quickly drag her eyes back to the colorful assembly. With no older brothers to take the crown, and Gavin the son of lesser nobility, she'd long resigned herself that the romantic dreams of childhood would have to remain buried.

Talianna did her best to smooth the furrow of worry from her brow, smile, and look like she was enjoying the festivities. *Stay focused, Tali.*

ONCE DINNER WAS OVER, the tables were cleared away and the dancing began. Gavin moved from the edge of the dais to a place near the wall as servants began circulating through the hall with platters of sweets and trays of hot and cold drinks. He ignored the buzz of conversations around him, keeping his eyes on Talianna as she made her way up and down the dance floor with one partner after another. After one rather rigorous reel, she cast an imploring glance in his direction. He ignored it, turning instead to examine the guard at the door. While they'd danced together at smaller events, it wouldn't be proper for him to take up a dance while other higher-ranked noblemen were present.

A woman's voice startled him from his contemplation. "Good evening, Milord."

He looked up in surprise. The speaker was one of the Treluthi-an ladies who had come with the ambassador and been stranded in the storm. Her auburn curls were piled high on her head in the courtly style, and her emerald-colored dress revealed far too much bosom for someone of her advancing age and apparent status.

"Good evening," he answered politely, keeping an eye out for Talianna as she proceeded down the line of dancers.

"Not dancing tonight?"

"Not I, no." He smiled. "I'm not much of a dancer."

"Oh!" She pressed a hand to her chest, surprise unconvincingly painting her heavily adorned features. "But you're so light on your feet, so alert!"

A nagging feeling pinged in the back of Gavin's head. "I'm all left feet on a dance floor. I'm afraid I'd bring you little enjoyment as a partner." He gave a slight bow in her direction before stepping away. "Enjoy the party."

The lady called an insult his way as he left, the shrillness in her words a counterpoint to the alarm coursing through his blood as he scanned the dance floor. The ballroom was still crowded with revelers, but Talianna and her partner had disappeared.

Where is she?

Cursing his own inattention, he stopped and searched the crowd for a glimpse of Talianna's burgundy dress. Finally, he spotted her sitting on a couch at the side of the hall, rubbing an ankle and laughing with her dance partner.

Relief flooded through him with a huffed laugh. "Those heels will never stop causing trouble."

Only now aware that his hand had gone to its bejeweled hilt, Gavin released his dagger. Conscious of a few curious stares, he resumed position against the wall to watch Talianna's interactions with the other nobleman. Based on the steady tightening of her jaw, he assumed the conversation was beginning to take a frustrating turn. It was no surprise when she reached up to fiddle with her tiara—their private signal for him to rescue her from whatever uncomfortable conversation she'd been trapped in.

His boots clicked against the floor as he walked over. "Your Royal Highness, I was told that your father wished to speak with you."

She looked up from her conversation with a radiant smile. "Oh! Gavin, thank you. Lord Baldric, may I present Sir Gavin of Andel."

Gavin bowed courteously to the man, whose chin seemed in danger of disappearing into his neck. The lord returned the bow with barely enough courtesy to honor the princess's introduction. His nose wrinkled as he said, "Andel? I've never heard of it."

Gavin chuckled. "Few have. It's a small barony, which is why I choose to stay at court."

"Don't you find it difficult to split your responsibilities?"

He shrugged. "My father still lives, and my older brother oversees our holdings at his side. Besides, my duty is here." He bowed to the lord again before returning his attention to Talianna. "My lady? Your father?"

With a practiced sigh, Talianna accepted his offered hand. Her fingers were warm in his as she took a moment to balance evenly in the high-heeled shoes. "Yes, my own duty calls. Lord Baldric, thank you for your courtesy."

The man bowed genteelly. "The pleasure was mine, Your Highness."

They walked away, Talianna looking up gratefully after a few steps. "Thank you for saving me. He was very irritating." A tinge of sarcasm crept through her voice, unusual for a court event. "He seems not to understand why the heir to the throne would rather spend her days studying diplomacy than having more maidenly pursuits."

"The pleasure is mine." He glanced away to see the nobleman already making for one of the beverage tables. "Though, you might consider speaking with your father, to keep up appearances."

"Yes, of course." She stopped and flexed her ankle gingerly. "I need a break before dancing more, anyway."

They joined the king and ambassador on the dais as the music began for another dance. Talianna sank into her chair with a relieved smile. Gavin excused himself, slipping to the rear of the platform and away from the monarch's direct gaze. In matters regarding Talianna's father, he preferred not to be seen as anything other than a dutiful servant. Kind to Talianna the man might be, but Gavin knew him to be so determined to do the right thing by his people that he wouldn't hesitate to remove anyone who might run the risk of distracting her from her responsibilities.

Like he did thirteen years ago. I wonder if he even remembers that day?

The royals and Treluthian ambassador exchanged pleasantries as the dancers moved through the formations of a gavotte. As the music ended, a servant approached with a tray of cups and offered them to the king.

"Ah, thank you." Talianna's father smiled at the man and lifted a cup from the tray. "Anyone else?"

Talianna nodded, also taking a glass. "Some of these pieces are quite fast. It's tiring!"

The servant excused himself with a nod and turned away. Out of the corner of his eye, Gavin noticed the man directing his steps toward the doors leading to the courtyard—not the kitchens. He took a half step backwards, keeping his eye on the servant. There was something suspicious about the man's manner as he crossed the dance floor. A tightness in his shoulders, perhaps, or a sharpness in his gaze as he looked back at the dais.

Sudden fear clenched in Gavin's gut. Grabbing the sleeve of the guard next to him, he ordered, "Stop that servant going out the doors."

The man's eyes widened as he obeyed, running toward the exit. Gavin looked back at the group on the dais. The king was still laughing over some joke with the ambassador and hadn't noticed the commotion behind him. Talianna's laugh fell on Gavin's ears like a warning bell as she lifted her goblet.

"Milady." Gavin lunged toward her, his voice building to a shout as Talianna sipped from her drink. "Milady, stop!"

Talianna had no time to respond before Gavin knocked the goblet away from her lips. It shattered on the dais floor, sending shards of crystal and a splatter of crimson across the polished stone. "Gavin, what…"

"Majesty, don't touch yours!" Gavin exclaimed, throwing an urgent hand in her father's direction.

Guards were breaking from their positions all around the ballroom, running out the doors with alarm stamped across their faces. The dancers closest to the dais faltered, stopping to look up with concern and confusion as her father demanded, "What is the meaning of this?"

Gavin grabbed her hands and pulled her to her feet, away from the table and away from the spilled drink. His green eyes found hers, as serious as the day he'd sworn his oath. "Princess, how much of your drink did you have?"

"Only a few sips, why?" Worry spiraled in her stomach.

He cast a dangerous glance at the door. "It might be nothing. I—I hope it's nothing. Don't drink anything else, all right?"

"All right."

Gavin squeezed her hands before letting go, his dark blue tunic remaining in the corner of her eye as he stepped to the back of the dais. Others of the king's guard were clustering around, their voices low and urgent as the sounds of the party swelled once more in the rest of the ballroom. The Treluthian ambassador had begun arguing with one of his men at the opposite end of the dais, their words too lost in the background noise for her to make out.

Talianna straightened her shoulders and smoothed her expression as her father turned from reassuring one of the other dignitaries and came to rest a hand upon her arm.

"Your captain may have overreacted. At least, I hope he has." He shot a concerned glance in Gavin's direction before asking, "Are you all right?"

"Yes, I think so." She smiled up at him, blinking as the gold embroidery on his tunic threw spots of light into her eyes. "Don't worry, Father, I'm fine."

"You're sure?"

Talianna nodded, but the movement slowed and changed to a frown as the faint spots kept dancing in her vision. She shook her head slightly, but the sparkling spots didn't dissipate. "Papa, something feels odd."

A tremor sped up her legs, building to a shudder as it ran through her body. Her father's voice blurred and fuzzed through her mind as his hand moved to her shoulder.

What's he saying? What's happening?

"Papa? Something is wrong." Her mouth felt heavy, her tongue tingly. "Something…" Talianna's words trailed into oblivion as a blue tunic flashed through her periphery and strong arms surrounded her. Above and around her, people were shouting, Gavin's voice strongest over all of them. She fought to answer him, or cry out, but her voice dissolved into incomprehensible sound. Darkness closed in.

Pandemonium spread through the palace at the speed of lightning, leaving all within dazed and confused as rumors began flying. Outside, the winter storm raged as alarm bells rang, gates swung closed, and hands flew to weapons. Inside, the tall windows peered down upon a handful of blue-uniformed men traveling in tight ranks through side halls, one of them carrying an unconscious woman clad in burgundy and gold.

Had the windows been able to tell their tale to the winter winds, they would have spoken of a hand brushing wisps of raven hair away from a still face and of a whisper barely heard amid the commotion.

"Tali. Don't go, please. I'll never forgive myself if you die."

Several hours later, Gavin paced back and forth before the hearth in Talianna's sitting room. It was long after midnight, and he'd been roaming restlessly around the room ever since the doctor had arrived and barred him from Talianna's bedchamber. A few of the other men from the personal guard also ranged through the sitting room and the antechamber beyond, the tension in their bodies declaring how frustrating they, too, found the situation.

After an hour, Gavin stopped pacing and turned to his men.

"It's no use for all of us to be rattling around in here." He gestured outside, where alarm bells could still be heard beyond the howling wind. "Go join the others in the search. You can report to Lord Kelmar, and he'll direct you." His men looked up, their eyes brightening with the suggestion as he added, "Keep your eyes and ears open and report anything you find to me or to the duke. I'll send someone to find you if anything happens here."

The other guards nodded their assent, a few of them clapping him on the shoulder as they left Talianna's suite. Gavin's second-in-command Tristan shook his head sympathetically as the anteroom door closed on the men's heels. "I had more peaceful nights at the Treluthian border."

Gavin nodded, the tension in his shoulders longing to be released in a fight of some kind. While peace with Treluthia had been declared long before he'd gained his knighthood, there had been enough skirmishes along the long, shared border between the two countries to test both nations' resolve—and their fighting forces' mettle. "The border was easy. At least there, we knew who we were fighting and why. This—" He shook his head. Peace was a more difficult battle than war, especially with unknown enemies sowing chaos at every turn. "Even fighting the wind would be better than this."

A creak from behind interrupted them as the doctor stepped through the door to Talianna's bedroom. Both Gavin and Tristan spun to face him, Gavin's voice overriding his subordinates'. "How is she?"

The doctor gave him a weary smile. "She's had a difficult few hours, but she'll be all right. Is there any word yet on who did this?"

"Not yet." Tristan gave a grim look toward the door. "Though,

I expect that'll change soon. The whole guard's been roused, not that it does our lady any good."

"At least she'll recover." The doctor nodded to Gavin. "Your quick thinking saved her." Gavin frowned and looked away as the man added, "I know you're worried; would you like to come sit with her?"

"I would. Thank you."

With the doctor's hand at his elbow, Gavin stepped into the bedchamber. Several assistants in white aprons stood near Talianna's four-poster bed, shifting pillows and tucking the covers around her. The princess laid as still as a statue, her face almost as pale as the neckline of her shift. Seeing her so vulnerable made his footsteps falter in a way that no deadly threat ever had.

One of Talianna's ladies-in-waiting stopped brushing the gown the princess had worn at the Midwinter Ball. She crossed the room to pull a chair to the bedside. "I realize it looks bad, but she's only sleeping," the woman murmured. Like most of the other courtiers waiting outside, she was still wearing her festive attire. "She was asking where you were, earlier." The woman gave him an encouraging smile. "Talk to her. Even if she can't respond, she'll know you're here."

"Thank you." Taking the seat, Gavin wrapped one of Talianna's hands in both of his. Her eyes flickered, face ghastly pale against her pillow. "Will anyone mind that I'm here? Propriety—the king—"

The doctor smiled, wrinkles making his skin pouch around his eyes. "Don't worry. All I know is that the princess's guardian refused to abandon his charge, even in her sickroom." He returned to his work, leaving Gavin holding Talianna's hand.

Hours later, Gavin stretched and stood up. Talianna still slept, more peaceful now that the doctor's medicines had taken effect. Morning light filtered past the curtains of the sitting room as he re-emerged from the bedchamber. Most of the hangers-on had left when they heard the princess would recover, and only a few of his men remained in the antechamber. "Any news?" he asked Tristan.

A twist at the corner of his comrade's mouth heralded the news. "They got him—*and* he talked." Worry lines creased at the edges of his eyes as he looked past Gavin toward Talianna's room. "You're not going to believe this, but the princess wasn't the intended target. His Majesty was."

Gavin swore under his breath. "It was an accident?"

Tristan nodded grimly. "Collateral damage, they're saying."

Gavin's hand tensed, about to go to where his sword normally sat against his hip. "Whomever 'they' are, they need to watch their tongues. That's their future queen they're talking about." He gave a shake of his head. "I came out here to ask if you could stay with her for a bit so I could go change. Maybe now I need to go hit someone while I'm at it."

Tristan clapped a hand on his shoulder. "Go do what you need to."

Gavin ducked through the servants' door with a few words of thanks and hurried down a single flight of stairs to his own quarters. Hastily changing out of his fancy clothes, he dressed according to comfort. He retrieved his sword from the armor rack and fastened it securely at his waist. The sheath of a wrist knife tightened around his right arm, and his hunting knife balanced his sword on the opposite hip. Armed, he collected a book and ink bottle from his bedside table and left the room. He was about to return to Talianna's room when his footsteps slowed.

Collateral damage? Her? He shook his head. *I can't go back in there until I calm down.*

The wind had begun abating outside as Gavin directed his steps to a lesser-known chapel on the ground floor of the palace. Today, with priests gathered in the main chapel praying for Talianna's safety, the place was deserted. His boots made quiet echoes in the vaulted space, candles flickering behind the altar as he sat on one of the front benches.

He sat in silence for several minutes, contemplating the altar and what it symbolized. Eventually, his senses calmed enough for him to open the book he'd brought from his room. A handful of pages in the back listed every time Talianna had been in mortal danger since he had taken over command of the men in charge of her protection.

The hunting accident, when her horse almost threw her. The riot in barony Eland. Even with the gravity of the situation, he had to smirk at one entry. *That poisoned perfume someone gave her…too bad for them that she hates the smell of lilies of the valley.* The levity left his thoughts as he uncapped the ink. Dipping a pen, he wrote in careful script the details of this most recent incident. *Even when she's not the target, she's still in danger.*

Setting the journal aside for the ink to dry, he got up from the pew and knelt at the prayer rail in front of the altar. The words of his oath fell into the silence. "I, Gavin of Andel, do solemnly swear to guard the princess Talianna to the fullest of my ability. May the blows of those who seek to cause her harm fall upon my head. May her enemies be my enemies, her danger my danger, and her life my life. This do I swear, until my king releases me from my oath or I perish in the fulfillment of my duty."

It's not a light promise. He shivered as the words sent a ripple of conviction through his heart. *I almost failed her last night. I can't afford to let that happen again.*

3

FLIGHT

TALIANNA RECOVERED QUICKLY FROM her illness, though the incident left her with even more determination to excel in her duties as heir. She'd already spent most of her time each week in study, but that occupation now grew to encompass every free moment. As spring budded into summer, she spent hours poring over books on history and politics, talking with her advisors, and researching the countries surrounding her realm.

"Father's health isn't the best," she confided in Gavin one afternoon as he walked with her from the council room to the library. "He doesn't say much, but I know he's worried that there won't be much time before all of this lands on my shoulders." Her shoulders slumped, and she reminded herself to straighten them. "I want so badly to rule well and to live up to everyone's expectations, and, and—oh, just to do this *right*."

"You'll do things right," he reassured her. "You're certainly studying enough."

Gavin's presence was a constant amid the study and meetings, broken only when she met with her father in private each week. The weekly audience had been something she dearly looked forward to as a child, when they could speak at length about games, playfellows, and Talianna's most recent interests; things she supposed ordinary fathers and daughters discussed every day. As her responsibilities as heir to his throne had increased, so too did the seriousness of the weekly conversations, until they now resembled more councils of strategy than the easy companionship she'd once enjoyed. And since Midwinter, the topic of conversation now drifted more toward the subject of her betrothal; a subject she could only answer with the bitter-tasting platitude: "I'm contemplating it."

In truth, each time the subject turned to marriage, the pressure in her mind increased. There were several men whose bloodlines were aristocratic enough and who possessed the academic and personal qualities necessary, yet the choice never settled in her heart.

You're being sentimental, she chided herself one afternoon while on a rare walk in the rose gardens. The audience with her father that morning had seen him reminding her yet again of his wishes, and this time with a deadline attached. *Father wants this matter settled before my twenty-first birthday, and there are plenty of candidates he would deem worthy. I ought to simply select someone who'll do his best for our people and leave it at that.*

She huffed a sigh into the fragrant air. *I don't want it to end like that, though.* Memories passed through the edge of her mind; of the sound of her parents' laughter as they'd played with her in this very garden. *They had something special with each other, before Mother's illness took her mind.* Talianna trailed her fingers down the velvet petals of a blush rose. *If I could have my wish, I'd be able to choose someone who wasn't only good for our people, but who made me laugh the way Mother made Father laugh.*

GAVIN STAYED AT TALIANNA'S side as much as he could over the months of recovery and study. Although the kingdom had been quiet since the events of Midwinter, he could feel the growing tension as her birthday drew closer. Peace still held sway, but a diplomatic iciness had descended over the court as relations with Treluthia grew increasingly strained. As the first days of summer broke over the land, Gavin received a summons to the king's council room.

Leaving Talianna in the library with trusted men to keep watch, he hurried to the council chamber. The interior corridors of the palace were dark and quiet, far from the gold-touched gardens where Talianna occasionally spent an afternoon with her ladies-in-waiting. He stopped outside the room and took a moment to adjust his uniform and compose himself before nodding to the guards outside the door.

"I'm ready."

One of them pounded twice on the door before opening it. "Good luck, Sir."

It was evident from first glance that this meeting would be of a serious nature. The king sat at one end of the table. His face was in a composed expression very much like the royal persona Talianna donned for public events. The Duke of Kelmar, Gavin's commander and overseer of the personal guards for king and queen, sat at the monarch's right. Others of the king's advisors occupied chairs around the table and swelled the room almost beyond its capacity. That number alone would have indicated the gravity of this meeting, but the expressions on the men's faces confirmed his growing suspicions. *This isn't a regular security briefing. It's a council of war.*

"Sir Gavin, thank you for taking time out of your duties to

attend us," the king said from the head of the room. "I trust the princess is well?"

Gavin came to attention, one hand going to his sword hilt in salute. "The princess is in excellent health and spirits, Majesty."

"I am glad to hear it." There was something akin to a smile about the monarch's face for a moment as he gestured to a seat at the foot of the table. "Please, sit. Our discussion may be of some length."

Gavin quietly took his seat and did his best to calm his quaking nerves. Most of the other nobles gave him dismissive looks, but Lord Kelmar gave him a reassuring half-smile as Talianna's father addressed the room. "Thank you all for being here today. I know it's difficult to assemble this many of us, so I won't waste your time." The king paused before continuing, his words those of a man who intended his audience to give him their full attention. "With the events of Midwinter, and the growing unrest elsewhere in the country, it's becoming apparent that our enemies are becoming more and more brazen in their attempts to undermine our security."

Heads nodded around the room, Gavin's among them. They'd traced the would-be kingslayer to a malcontent son of a provincial duke, whose perceived claim on the throne had to be traced through several branches of the family tree. Gavin hadn't known for certain if the man's decision to strike the king had been influenced by any specific enemy, but the sheer audacity, combined with the reports of chaos brewing in other corners of the land, made for convincing evidence of outside interference.

Chaos, his old battle master had once said. *Sow chaos behind your opponent's lines, and they'll be powerless against you.*

"The most recent strike against me endangered my daughter's

life," the king continued. "I'd hoped that with increased precautions, she'd be able to remain at my side until her coming of age later this year. But with each new threat comes the possibility of her simply being in the wrong place at the wrong moment, like she was at Midwinter. Threats against my life are one thing, but now my daughter's life is in danger." The king frowned, his composed demeanor cracking enough for Gavin to recognize the same heart-stopping fear that filled him with each new threat against Talianna. "She needs to leave."

The words left Gavin's mouth numb with fear. "H-how long have you been planning this?" Everyone turned to look at him with varying degrees of surprise as he stammered, "Why hasn't any mention been made until now?"

"We'd been discussing moving the princess to a safer location for several months, but the events surrounding and following Midwinter have made it clear." Lord Kelmar steepled his fingers over a pile of notes at the other end of the table. "The longer she stays here, the more danger she's in."

Gavin sat in stunned silence as the rest of the council carried on. Now that the urgency of their circumstances had been driven home, the room hummed with discussion—ranging from how to cover Talianna's absence at court to laying plans to isolate and address the sources of unrest elsewhere in the kingdom.

Finally, Gavin felt his mind clear enough to venture a question. "Has there been a decision on where Talianna will go for this period? I mean," he addressed the king. "Your Majesty, my men and I will go anywhere to ensure Her Highness's safety. Is there already a destination in mind?"

The king nodded at a framed map on the wall. "Fife Corbel."

Gavin turned to look as well, though he knew the layout of the country almost as well as he knew his own rooms. The palace lay in the top left corner, a great forest cutting a swath between it and the sunlit coastal regions to the southeast. From his remembrance, Fife Corbel lay on the coast, beyond the forest. "It's far enough, Milord, but why there?"

"The queen's brother, the Earl of Corbel, is Talianna's closest relative." Lord Kelmar ran his thumb down the edge of his stack of notes. "The princess spent summers there with Her Majesty, before the queen's illness became too severe to permit travel." He tilted his head at the map, the lamplight catching in a scar that marked his eyebrow. "It's far away, and not in a heavily traveled area. If we're careful in our secrecy, no one will know where she's gone until months later. By then, hopefully, we'll have contained the unrest enough for her to return home."

Gavin nodded, his mind churning with logistics, concerns, and burning worry. In the end, only one question floated to the top of his mind. "How soon?"

"Next week?" Talianna hadn't had to remind herself to keep her composure in years, but Gavin's news was enough to make her jaw drop. She looked around to make sure no one had over-heard her outburst. Fortunately, her ladies had wandered across the grass to take shelter from the sun under the rose arbors and were certainly out of earshot. "So soon? With not even a word of warning?"

He tilted his head, and a spark flared in his green eyes; a brief concession that told her how frustrating the news had most likely been to him as well. "Lord Kelmar has a point. This entire plan is based in secrecy, and every day spent here only increases the chance of someone reaching you." He crossed his arms and leaned against the edge of the fountain, sunlight throwing a gleam from his sword hilt into her eyes. In the direct sun, his hair looked almost the same gold color as it had been when they were children. "I wanted to leave right away, but your father wants you here for the Flower Bridge Festival."

"I understand why," Talianna said after a moment of thought. "It would be immediately suspicious if I didn't appear with him at the celebrations. If we leave afterwards, it'll take days or even weeks before anyone notices I'm gone. Ordinarily, Mother would be the one to open the festival with him, but—" She looked across the garden, ashamed at the sudden prickling of tears. "Mother doesn't remember what day of the week it is, let alone when holidays are."

Gavin pulled a handkerchief from his tunic pocket and offered it to her. "I'm sorry. I didn't realize…" His voice trailed off as she wiped her eyes.

"It's all right. I don't even think about it most of the time; it just catches me unexpectedly." Talianna cleared her throat. Gavin had accompanied her on her last visit but had waited outside the private sitting room where her mother spent most of her days. "She remembers my name, but time isn't the same for her anymore. When she saw me last, she wanted to know where my nursie was."

He gave a low whistle. "I didn't realize it'd become so bad. That does explain why your father doesn't want us to leave until after the festival."

"Yes." The word stuck in her throat. "It makes sense. Did they say how we're getting to my uncle's holding?"

Gavin frowned. His eyes hadn't stopped roving the gardens since he'd given her the handkerchief. "The most direct and secret way possible: right through the woods."

Talianna followed his line of sight toward the edge of the garden, where the gardens were divided from tended parkland by a wrought-iron gate. Far beyond, the woods swelled in undulating waves of deep green and brown. "Stories say those woods are alive." She grinned. "And that banshees and witches walk between the trees." She tore her gaze away from the distant trees to look directly at Gavin. "Is it really dangerous? I mean, I've heard some of the girls talk…"

He snorted. "All girls talk, but some of your ladies have made it an art form." One of his eyebrows quirked as he added, "They'll hear a hunter's tale that he got from his cousin's father, and between embroidery circles and hawking parties turn it into a tale for the ages."

"I suppose that's true," she admitted. One or two of the younger girls among her ladies-in-waiting weren't the most well-read or burdened with much common sense, but their silliness was refreshing—soothing, even—after hours spent in the company of diplomats and scholars. "But really?" she asked as they got up and began walking under the arch that separated the rose garden from the rest of the grounds. "Is it dangerous?"

"Some parts of the forest are thick enough that we don't always know what passes unnoticed." Gavin raised an eyebrow, conceding, "I did hear a story when I was on the border, about how the trees moved of their own accord to block a raiding party." He shrugged. "The stories might not be too far off with the tales of old magic. But the security council was right: it is the fastest way to get to Fife Corbel, and we'll be able to make good time if we travel with a smaller group."

"If that's what they agreed on…" Talianna stopped to breathe in the perfume of the pink roses that tumbled over the archway. They'd played in this same garden as children, before duty had taken her to her studies and Gavin to training for knighthood.

Say goodbye, Talianna. Her nursie's voice floated through her ears as the sunlight gilded the edges of the rose leaves.

"I'll miss this place." She reached up to break the stem of one of the roses, tucking it into the laces on her bodice. "Even if it's only for a short while, I'll miss it."

Five nights later, a knock sounded on Gavin's door. Jerked from a sound sleep, he stumbled out of bed with a knife in hand and yanked open his bedroom door. "What's going on?"

Lord Kelmar leapt away from the threshold, the light from a lantern flaring and casting eerie shadows against the narrow corridor walls. "Shh! Stand down, it's only me."

Gavin warily relaxed his stance, lowering the knife. "What's happening?" The Flower Bridge Festival had only just concluded, and he and Talianna weren't due to leave for Fife Corbel for another several days. For that matter, he'd barely briefed the men who were to make up the remainder of the escort through the forest. "Is something wrong? The princess—"

"Is asleep. For now," the duke reassured him. "Though, you need to wake her at once." He passed a document to Gavin, the raised crimson and gold of the king's seal imprinted beneath its words. The shadows seemed to thicken around them as the man said grimly, "There's been a change of plans."

IN THE PALE MORNING light, a back gate of the stables opened onto mist. Talianna drew her hood farther around her face and buried her free hand in the folds of her mantle as she urged her horse into a trot. Ahead, Gavin guided his own horse deeper into the fog that cloaked the gate and shrouded the road leading to the forest.

"Your time and manner of leaving have become compromised," her father's advisor had warned them in the darkest hours preceding dawn. "His Majesty issued me new orders. You're to proceed at once to the eastern road and go as fast as you can to Fife Corbel. We'll send your possessions by caravan along a different route." The man's face had been drawn with worry, matched only by the tension in Gavin's face as the duke clasped his hand and commanded, "Guard her well. The fate of us all rests on your shoulders."

They'd dressed quickly in commoners' clothes, loaded plain saddlebags onto nondescript horses, and made their course for the eastern road. As the sun crested the edge of the trees and set every dewdrop aflame, Talianna reined her horse down to a walk alongside Gavin's. "What happened?"

He raked a hand through his blond hair before letting his hand drop to the hilt of a plain sword. "I briefed the men who were going to accompany us yesterday. They must've decided to bid the capital farewell in fine fashion, because the city guard arrested one of them overnight for causing a drunken disturbance. We're not sure who he might have spoken with over the course of the evening, and it could have been enough to compromise our plans." His jaw tensed. "And your father wanted absolute secrecy."

Talianna shook the hood of her cloak away from her forehead. "So they decided it was best we leave immediately?" She stared into the depths of the forest, sunbeams slicing through the trees as the sun climbed higher into the sky.

"Yes." He tightened his hands around his reins. "I don't like it either, but the orders came directly from your father. I have *some* amount of liberty to question my superiors, but not an order with the royal seal on it."

Talianna nodded. Her father's seal was practically an extension of himself; its appearance tantamount to hearing his voice directly. "Whatever happened must have disrupted more than just our departure," she said, half to herself and half to Gavin.

"I think so as well," he agreed, "I can't think of another reason they'd panic the way they did." His face flushed, and he half turned in the saddle to face her. "I mean—not panic. I don't think they panicked, it's just—"

She found herself laughing, letting go of the tension brought on by their hurried departure. "It's all right. I won't say anything." The surprised relief in Gavin's expression loosened more tightness from her shoulders as she asked, "It's how long of a journey? Three weeks?"

"It *was* three weeks the way we'd planned on traveling," Gavin corrected. "With only two of us, it'll be closer to a fortnight."

"Two weeks," she repeated. "Two weeks before I have to be the princess again."

He chuckled. "Be careful; you might forget how to wear the royal persona."

"Well, I doubt it'll go *that* far." She sighed. "I've had years to perfect it, after all." She shot him a piercing glance. "How long did it take you to realize it was a façade?"

Gavin shrugged, the set of his body in the saddle reminding her how much time he'd spent on different military campaigns prior to swearing his oath. "A few months. I walk behind you all the time, so it was easy to notice when you were getting ready for battle."

"Some days it feels like one," she admitted. "At least for right now, I don't have to worry about being the heir to the throne. I can just be…me. Just Tali." She flicked a hand in his direction. "You can use my old nickname, if you want. There's no one here to overhear, and I won't tell."

A grin caught the corner of Gavin's mouth. "I've never stopped calling you that in my head." He tipped his head back as sunlight filtered through the trees overhead, examining the canopy with eyes that reflected its green and gold hues. "We'd better speed up. Childhood nicknames aside, this adventure could still end in a way that neither of us would've imagined."

Gavin had never thought that a tension-filled departure could lead to such peace. Away from the palace, Talianna's royal persona steadily dissolved, until she seemed more like the girl she had once been. The bubbly side of her personality had returned by the end of the second day, and by the third evening, she was as talkative and cheerful as he remembered her being during childhood.

Keep your wits about you, he reminded himself on the third night, as they set up camp in a clearing beneath a spreading oak tree. *This may be a reprieve from the usual, but nothing has changed between you.* He cast a glance at Talianna as she collected fuel for their campfire. They'd donned simple clothes for traveling, but she made even a plain brown dress and wool cloak beautiful. *Once we're among nobles again, she'll be back to being the princess—and you have a duty to keep your heart from getting tangled into your common sense. There's too much at stake to get lazy now.*

He forced himself to look away and focus on their surroundings. This clearing was a little way away from the road, and he hoped the distance and obscurity would hide them from anyone who happened to be passing during the night. Previous travelers had thought similarly, and a blackened ring of rocks showed where someone had once lit a fire like the one he was now coaxing to life.

"Here." Talianna set a bundle of twigs and dry leaves beside him, brushing dirt from her hands as she knelt on the other side of the tiny circle. Her brow furrowed as she looked at the sky, visible in gaps where the treetops had not deigned to touch each other. "Is there a reason we stopped so early?"

Gavin sat back on his heels. Their interactions had grown much more familiar the farther into the woods they'd gotten, but he hadn't realized she'd learned his patterns for travel so quickly. "We're getting closer to the center of the forest." He glanced at the brambles that screened them from the path. This close, their thorns looked sharp as daggers. "I don't want to spend the night in the deepest part, so we'll get an early start tomorrow and push through the middle of the woods in one day."

He bent over the fire and carefully blew into the growing embers, then added a handful of dry leaves. They caught immediately, the sudden flare of light illuminating Talianna's face with a glow like the sun. She sat down, pulling in her legs and tucking her feet under her worn skirts. "Are you expecting something to happen?"

Gavin snapped a stick and tossed it into the fire. "I don't know, Tali," he admitted. Even if he'd have to eventually resume calling her by her full name, Talianna's childhood nickname warmed his heart each time he said it. "It's still another several days to the edge of the forest, and I don't know what we might encounter as we go. I said I didn't care about the stories they tell about these woods, but that doesn't change the fact that there *are* stories." He looked down, glad that the fire was warm enough to cover the flush spreading across his face. "It was easier to ignore them when I thought we'd have more men with us."

Talianna's thoughtful hum was loud enough to be heard over the soft crackling of the fire. "Then, what will we do?"

"Keep going." He snapped another stick and stabbed the ground with it. "Whatever reservations I had about our departure, your father's order still needs to be carried out. I'll deliver you safely to your uncle's fife; make no mistake about that. As to what we might encounter—" Gavin cut himself off. "I swore to protect you at the expense of myself, and I'll hold true to that oath even if there's no one to witness it. But if we *do* run into trouble, I need you to make me a promise."

"What promise?" Talianna looked up from the fire, and his heart beat faster at how its light turned her eyes amber and gold; the colors of the sun contained in a woman with all its brilliance.

"Whatever happens, you need to get out of this forest. If you can, stay hidden. If you can't, run." He crossed the campfire circle to take her hand like he had at Midwinter. "Please, Tali. Promise."

"I promise, of course." She smiled. "I'm certain you underestimate yourself, though."

That night, Gavin scaled the oak to discover a mossy hollow where several branches had grown together at the trunk. He laid Talianna's bedding in the depression, telling her, "It might be uncomfortable, but I'll feel better knowing you're above ground." He laid his blanket next to the dying fire, staring into the night sky long after Talianna had fallen asleep in her nest. Finally, Gavin fell into a restless sleep.

A creak woke him—not of a tree or animal, but of boots over rocks. Eyes open, staring into the darkness, Gavin wondered how long it was until dawn. The fire had burned down to coals, but he could make out several dark shapes creeping up on him through the undergrowth. Lying still, he closed his eyes to slits. *Better to make them think I'm alone and unaware than lose the element of surprise.* Inside, his mind was spinning with possibilities and plans. Were they highwaymen, or something worse? Who could have learned about their departure?

"Shh." The deep, unfamiliar voice came from above him. "Check his gear."

Gavin gritted his teeth as his scabbard—laid with the hilt resting near his arm—slid away. Another voice, rough with whispering, muttered, "Army issue. You sure this is the knight?"

"They said he was." It was a different voice than the first. One of the horses nickered, and Gavin opened his eyes to barest slits as one of the dark figures moved to rummage through a saddlebag. "No livery on the horses, either. Doesn't matter; I still think this is our man."

"He's alone, though," another voice whispered. "If this is him, where is *she?*"

A chill that had nothing to do with the unyielding ground sped through his limbs. *They know.*

"Don't know," the first voice replied. "Not that it matters who dies first." Gavin sensed movement close, and his muscles tensed at the sound of steel sliding free of a sheath. "'Sides, she won't last long without him protectin' her."

Panic flashed through his mind as someone loomed over him. In an instant, Gavin rolled to his feet and freed his hunting knife. He stabbed upwards into the jaw of the man who had been about to kick him awake, then yanked down. Shouts rang out, and the man collapsed with a gurgle as Gavin stumbled to get his back to the oak. *Stay quiet, Tali.*

Someone else grabbed his arm, and he blindly swiped with his knife. It caught, and the man backed up with a curse. Yanking another blade from his boot, Gavin settled into a crouch, his eyes adjusting to the darkness as the bandits circled him. The man he had stabbed writhed on the ground for a few seconds before lying still with a rattling breath.

"Guess I underestimated you," the first man said. "That won't happen again. Grab him, lads."

Gavin heard the noise behind his left shoulder too late, as another bandit leapt at him from behind the oak. Others piled on, and he found himself immobile under the sheer weight. His knives twisted out of his hands before something heavy hit the back of his head. The blow dizzied him, and he was only dimly aware as the bandits bound his limbs before loading him onto the horse. Someone thrust a sack over his head, and the horse began moving. His only thought as they began making their way deeper into the forest was that Talianna had remained undiscovered. *Run, Talianna. Do as I said and run!*

4

DEFIANCE

STICKS CRACKED AND RUSTLED as Talianna slid down from the oak. *They didn't see me. Why didn't they see me?* She leaned against the tree as her limbs shook with adrenaline and fear. After a moment, the pressure of the bark against her skin had settled her tremors enough for understanding to come to mind. "They never looked up," she whispered. She twisted to press her forehead against the oak's craggy bark. "They never looked up!"

Something at once calm and fierce stirred inside her chest. *I can't leave Gavin.* The memory of his tear-filled eyes stirred unexpectedly at the back of her mind. Her nursemaid's voice had been sympathetic but unmoving that day, when Talianna's childhood had ended. *I've left him before, and look where it got us.*

Talianna pulled the edges of her cloak tightly around herself and set off toward the distant sounds of men talking and laughing, praying every step of the way that this was courage speaking, and not foolishness.

LIGHT STUNG GAVIN'S EYES as someone pulled the sack off his head. He looked around dizzily as the men pulled him off the horse and pushed him to the ground near the center of a ring of massive old trees. The ground here was trodden hard and bare, and a fire burned brightly in the center of the ring. Other men like the ones who'd captured him could be seen around the circle. Their clothes were plain, serviceable, and worn, but all bore weapons with the familiarity of those accustomed to using them. Even at this late hour, many were awake; checking gear, playing dice, or talking with their fellows. A man with broad shoulders and an old army-issue sword crossed the circle to demand, "What's going on here?"

One of the bandits prodded Gavin with the toe of his boot. "Sir, we found this one in the oak clearing. He fits the description and there were two horses, but he was alone."

The man made a frustrated noise. "I don't recall saying any-thing about bringing them back here. How clear did I need to be?"

The outlaw shook his head, a whine creeping through his voice. "We were going to take care of things, but he turned out to have a way wi' a knife."

"Sir, he got Devin," another man said. "He's dead."

"Now that *is* a surprise. I can't let that go unpunished." The outlaw leader looked more appraisingly at Gavin. "Where are you from? Who are you?"

Just protect Talianna. "Treluthian border," Gavin lied. "And I'm only passing through. I didn't mean to cause trouble."

"Hmmm." The man turned away, and for a moment, Gavin thought his ruse had worked. Then, the outlaw spun to slam a boot into Gavin's stomach. "Don't lie to me! Who are you!?"

Gavin caught his breath with a shudder and shook his head. "I'm just a traveler!"

The outlaw leader's hand went to his sword hilt. "I said—"

"Sir?" One of the bandits held out the wrist knife he'd taken when binding Gavin's hands. "He did have this on him."

The leader snatched the small knife from his subordinate, his irritated expression swiftly changing to interest at the sight of the coat of arms stamped on the underside of the sheath. "The White Falcon," he breathed, turning a triumphant look at Gavin. "Barony Andel?"

Gavin's heart sank.

The bandit leader crouched to look Gavin in the eye, a misshapen grin spreading across his face. "Then you must be *Sir Gavin* of Andel, guard commander to Princess Talianna. Do you know how many people are after your skin, and how much they're willing to pay?"

"Not nearly as many as are after my lady's," Gavin answered. "You don't seem surprised to have met us."

"Well, not 'us' just yet." The man stood up and shook the closest man by his tunic front before releasing him with a shove. "Didn't you bastards search the campsite?"

The bandit stumbled backwards as one of the others said, "We did, Sir! There was no one else there!"

"Aye, that's likely. They warned that he might do something like this. You! And you!" The outlaw stabbed a hand in the direction of several of the men. "Get back to that campsite. Search it *properly* this time." The outlaw leader bent down to Gavin once more. "Where did you hide her? Tell us how to find her, and you'll live. The ones that hired us needn't find out, and I'll even overlook you killing one of my men." His voice grated an octave lower. "Refuse, and you die."

Gavin choked back fear and glared silently at the bandit leader.

The quiet strained at the edges of the clearing before the outlaw's stare broke with a grim sigh. "Going to be stubborn? So be it." The man stood up and snapped his fingers. Before Gavin had the chance to react or pull away, two of the others had hauled him to his feet and were yanking him to where a set of sturdy posts and shackles stood anchored in the ground.

Pure terror shot through Gavin's veins. He dug his heels into the ground, wrenching his shoulder free for a moment before his captors' grips tightened on his arms. The ropes binding his wrists loosened, and his shirt tangled around his head before being ripped away. Every instinct he possessed screamed for him to fight back, escape, run, as cold iron snapped shut around his wrists.

I'm sorry, Tali. At least I can buy you some time. He set his jaw and focused on the darkness beyond the circle of trees, his oath reverberating in his mind. *May the blows of those who seek to cause her harm fall upon my head. This do I swear, until my king releases me—or I perish.*

Talianna crouched in the shadows on the far side of the clearing as the guards dragged Gavin to the posts. Her breath caught as he stared, wide-eyed and fearful, into the darkness that surrounded her. *Surely, he doesn't know I'm here. He can't.*

Her fingers clutched at the dirt as another bandit walked up holding a coiled whip. *He told me to run. I promised.* Fear froze her hands into fists and her knees to the ground. *I can't.*

The bandit leader walked around to face Gavin and said something she couldn't hear. A spark of defiance flared, thawing her limbs as her friend spat in the outlaw's face. The man reeled back in surprise before backhanding him viciously. Gavin's head snapped to the side, his face contorting in pain. *He's doing this for me. I'm not worthy of that.*

Worthy.

The word went through her heart faster than any assassin's arrow; every connotation of noble birth, good social standing, and courtly manners disappearing into shocking clarity. *The most worthy man I know has been standing at my back this whole time.*

Talianna clapped her hands over her mouth as the man with the whip brought it hissing through the air toward his victim. She closed her eyes before the blow fell, dirt-covered fingers stifling her own scream.

GAVIN WAS NOT A stranger to pain—no one who'd earned a knighthood was. Still, he fought hard to stop himself from shrieking as the lash cracked across his back. He gritted his teeth and tried not to bite his tongue as another blow came. And another. Another. A ribbon of blood trickled down his spine, warm against his skin as he tried not to scream. The seconds stretched, broken only by shuddering pain and the cracking of the lash before the outlaw leader demanded, "Where is she? Tell me!"

He focused his breathing, calmed his shaking limbs, and said nothing. The man sneered and answered, "It's your life. Be stubborn if you wish." He waved his hand and another blow slammed into Gavin's back.

Talianna hadn't closed her eyes for long. The sound that the lash made as it curled through the air forced her to stay riveted to the scene unfolding in the clearing. Gavin slumped between the posts, his back bloodied and crossed with lash marks. The bandit leader hadn't stopped his attempts at convincing his prisoner to give up her whereabouts—a fact confirmed with a shouted demand that sent a white-hot bolt of terror through her chest. Each time, her friend rallied to challenge his captor, but even Talianna could see it was fast becoming a losing battle.

Can't I stop this? The thought sent a burst of heat through her heart, terror combining with the urge to throw herself from the bushes and into the circle of light. Even as her muscles tensed to obey, sudden cold arrested her movement. A chilly voice echoed at the back of her head, the same painfully correct void that greeted her each time she hesitated in carrying out her royal duties. *You have your own oath to fulfill. If you surrender, your people are lost.*

Talianna forced her eyes shut on the tears as the cold closed over her breaking heart.

I can't. Forgive me.

Her eyelids snapped open as the sounds from the clearing paused. The other bandits' faces had grown drawn and uncertain as their leader once again addressed Gavin's swaying form. This time, the questions were met with silence, and Talianna knew that silence was the only form of rebellion he could muster.

Suddenly, the outlaw's countenance changed from contempt

to rage. He wheeled around, and Talianna could hear the order even from across the clearing. "Kill him!"

No. NO!

The lashes redoubled through the air, and for the first time, Gavin screamed.

5

FAILURE

It didn't take long

Not even a few minutes after the bandit leader had given his merciless order, a hush fell over the clearing. Talianna took a shaky breath, her jaw aching from holding in her own distress as the man with the whip stepped closer to Gavin. He'd stopped screaming a heartbreaking minute before, and his head hung limply between bloodstained shoulders.

The bandit straightened, the quiet in the clearing so profound that his words to his commander could be heard even from the darkness beyond. "I think he's finished, Sir. What are your orders?"

Keys flashed in the firelight. "Dump him in the woods. Then get back here as fast as you can." The outlaw leader glared into the darkness, the set of his shoulders betraying no remorse at what he'd just witnessed. "We've got a princess to catch."

The sound of keys jangling against the shackles was enough to send her heartbeat skyrocketing with urgency. *He's dead.* Talianna caught her breath with a muffled sob. *He's dead, and it's my fault. It doesn't matter what happens now; I'm never going to forgive myself for this.*

She shrank away from the clearing as two other men came to help their comrade unlock the shackles around Gavin's wrists. He remained totally limp as they grabbed his arms and pulled him into the darkness less than fifty feet from where she crouched in the shelter of the bushes.

I have to know for certain. Swallowing her tears, she inched from beyond the bushes and slipped between the trees after them. Behind her, the noise from the bandit camp gradually increased, until it was the same constant rumble of voices that it had been before the harrowing events of the last hour.

The forest beyond the firelight shifted and settled in a thousand shadows, moonglow spilling through gaps in the trees to paint clearings with occasional patches of silvery light. A cluster of birch trees surrounded one such open patch of sky, the undergrowth broken where an old tree had fallen and decayed. Talianna halted as soon as the bandits did. The adrenaline from earlier was wearing off in the dark, quiet depths of the forest, and she could feel tears once more threatening to burst out and reveal her presence. She pressed herself against the smooth bark of one of the trees and peered past its trunk as the man in the lead said, "This ought to be far enough."

The others dropped Gavin's arms, the moonlight casting their shadows in jagged black shapes along the trampled grass. One of them shook his head. "It's a shame. He had spirit."

"Shut up," one of the others said. "He killed one of ours."

"I'm just saying—" He stopped. "Cor. Look."

Talianna's eyes widened as the first man dropped to a knee beside Gavin. The pale moonlight was barely enough to illuminate his bloody, motionless form as the bandit turned him over, but after a moment, Talianna realized what the bandit had noticed. Gavin's chest spasmed once, twice, then subsided into shallow breaths.

Sudden, sharp hope streaked through Talianna's chest. She

wrapped her hands around the tree trunk in an effort to stay upright as the bandits took a startled step back.

"Holy Mother," one exclaimed. "He's stronger than I thought!"

"He's alive?"

"Not for long." Steel rasped from its sheath as the second bandit drew a dagger.

Just as he was about to bring the blade across Gavin's throat, one of the others grabbed his arm. "Leave him," he commanded. "He's finished anyway. Whether he stopped breathing at camp or stops breathing here, it's all the same thing."

"But he killed—"

Don't touch him! Talianna's hands tightened on the tree trunk, everything within her building in a silent scream as tears streamed down her face. *Leave him alone!*

The bark beneath her hands flexed, and everything around her seemed to shake. A deep groan reverberated through the ground as the birch leaves rustled menacingly overhead.

All three men cursed and dropped into startled crouches. "Sorcery," the one with the dagger whispered.

Talianna snatched her hands from the tree as if the bark had burned her. *Did I do that?*

The man who'd expressed pity for Gavin bolted first, the dingy white of his shirt disappearing the way they'd come. The other two straightened, the one with the dagger replacing it in his belt as his comrade whispered, "No one says anything about this."

"Right." He took a slow step away, and Talianna caught a glimpse of the whites of his eyes as he turned toward the path. "Not a word."

The rustling of ferns marked the bandits' retreat, and within a few moments the clearing was still once more. Talianna waited with her heartbeat thundering in her ears, until she was certain no one was returning. With a frightful glance split evenly between trees and path, she stepped into the patch of moonlight and hurried to Gavin, lying in the shelter of one of the birch trees. She sank to her knees, feeling under his chin for a heartbeat. After long moments, a weak, rapid pulse thumped against her fingers.

"You're alive." Whatever other words she'd meant to say dissolved into tears. "You stupid fool; why did you do it? Oath or no oath, no one in their right mind would say I'm worth something like this!"

Worth protecting. Worth dying for. Talianna swallowed her tears and took a deep breath. The moonlight shifted over Gavin's face as she looked at him with new understanding.

"I got you into this," she told him. "Now I'm going to get you out." Talianna peered at the sky. Even in the short amount of time they'd been in this grove, the darkness had shifted into the thin light of false dawn. The mental image of this corner of the country—memorized over hours of studying maps and trade routes—leaped to the forefront of her mind. From what she could remember, their destination lay east of the woods—opposite of where the moon was fast sinking.

Talianna's hands flew to the clasp of her cloak. Laying it on the ground, she managed to roll Gavin to his stomach and onto the fabric. The sight of the damage done to his back and shoulders—dirt and blood creating dark shadows across ruined skin—was enough to send a fresh rush of tears to her eyes. She forced down the emotion with a fierce shake of her head, the cold of her royal nature closing over her. *Preparing for battle, he called it. Perhaps it's exactly what I need.*

Wrapping the ends of the cloak around her hands, Talianna

began hauling the improvised stretcher in the direction opposite the sinking moon. It didn't take long before dawn began to lighten the woods with a misty grey glow, and the first birds began trilling in the treetops. Gavin barely stirred beyond the occasional moan, but Talianna could see that the movement was taking its toll on his unconscious body. Fresh blood was beginning to spread in dark patches across the fabric of the cloak, and his breathing had changed cadence from barely perceptible to labored and pained.

I can't keep moving him like this.

The forest had opened out onto the bank of a tiny stream, and Talianna halted their progress to rip a band of cloth from the hem of her underskirt. She knelt beside Gavin, her stomach churning with guilt at the sight of injuries now revealed in daylight. "I'm sorry," she whispered as she pressed the cloth into one of the worst gashes. "I'm not a healer; I don't know what else to do."

She glanced over her shoulder in the direction they'd come. There hadn't been any sight or sound of pursuit, and she could only hope that the bandits had gone searching for her in the wrong direction. "This is all my fault. I'm so sorry."

THE NOISE OF flowing water was the first thing to fall on Gavin's senses. He opened his eyes to the sight of a stream only a short distance away, its cheerful gurgling harmonizing with the steady drone of bees somewhere nearby. The golden light of true dawn illuminated everything, rapidly blurring as pain overwhelmed his vision. *How did I get here?*

Suddenly, he realized there was fabric under his face—torn, bloodstained fabric the same dark grey as Talianna's cloak. No sooner had the thought crossed his mind when a shadow fell across his face, and Talianna herself appeared.

"You're awake!" She dropped to her knees next to him, one hand going out to touch his shoulder—then stopping. In a heartbreaking moment, he understood what had happened.

"What are you doing here?"

Her eyes darted away from his. "I couldn't leave you alone. I followed you."

"You should have run!" He tried to get an arm underneath himself to sit up, but the motion sent a tearing sensation across his back and shoulders, and he collapsed with a groan. "They're looking for you."

"I know," Talianna said. "I'm not sure how far away we are, but I think they're looking for me at the campsite." Tears started pooling in her eyes. "I'm sorry—I tried to get us as far away as I could, but you're still bleeding, and I don't know what else to do."

He caught his breath as clarity struck. "You saw, didn't you?"

Talianna's voice cracked. "I saw everything."

Fabric rustled as she retreated to the edge of the stream, returning to offer him a dripping handkerchief. "Here. Rinse your mouth out."

This time, his limbs obeyed him. He struggled to an elbow and took the handkerchief, wincing as a metallic taste coated his tongue. It dissipated in the first drops of water, though nothing could erase the memory of blood filling his mouth. "Thank you," he whispered.

"Can I clean your face off?"

Gavin shook his head. "Let me."

She sat back on her heels as he carefully wiped his face. Even that slow movement was enough to send his hand shaking, and the cloth fell to the ground with a dull splat. "Sorry."

"It's—it's all right." She got up and went to soak the handkerchief again. His limbs kept tremoring until he was forced to resume lying on his stomach, face resting on a bent arm. Talianna set a hand to his forehead upon her return, a frown crossing her face as her fingers touched his skin. "You need a doctor."

"*You* need to leave," he insisted. "They're going to figure out soon enough that you're not at the campsite, and if they find you, they'll kill you." He caught his breath on the heels of a spurt of pain. "You have to leave me here and go on by yourself."

Talianna scowled at him. "Absolutely not."

"Tali—"

"No!" She dropped the cloth on the cloak next to him. "If they find you here, they'll finish what they started!"

"Started—finished—it's all the same thing." He forced himself to meet her eyes, hoping beyond all hope that none of the pain was showing through. "Trust me, Tali. You'll only waste time moving me, and it's not going to change the outcome."

"You don't understand," she insisted, her hands tensing in her lap. "I can't leave you here to die!"

"You have to! I'm replaceable—you aren't!" He struggled to sit, getting as far as an elbow before stopping with a pained gasp. Something warm ran down his shoulder as he said, "If you die, this country will tear itself apart. Forget whatever brought us together in the past; what matters now is the people who'll suffer if you're lost. We're on the verge of war as it is, and this could push us over the brink." His heartbeat pounded in his ears, breath growing ragged as he put as much adamance into his voice as he could. "You're meant to lead our people, but you can't do that if you're lying dead next to me!"

Talianna inhaled sharply as if something had stung her. The edge of her skirt brushed his skin as she got to her feet, that barest touch sending a red wash of pain across his vision. The logical part of his mind warned him with a certain solemnity that he was in shock; that soon his injuries would rob him of the ability to think clearly or take action to protect himself or anyone else. *She has to leave.*

Gavin raised his head as much as he could. Talianna was standing at the edge of the river, wisps of dark hair stirring in the breeze as the water rippled past. "Please, Tali," he whispered. "I wouldn't be able to bear it if you died too."

Talianna's shoulders bowed for a long moment. Then, as gradually as twilight snuffing the light from the sky, her posture changed. Her chin lifted, her spine straightened, and her hands closed into fists at her sides. When she finally turned to face him, the childhood friend he'd spent the last few days with was gone, replaced by the woman he'd sworn to protect with his life.

"All—all right," Talianna said, her voice wavering but growing stronger with each word. "I'll do as you say." Her eyes—all business, now—roved the landscape before settling on something behind him. "Can you hide under that bush?"

He turned his head gingerly. A cluster of elder bushes stretched almost to the water's edge, the space beneath their frothy blossoms clear of grass and shaded from the sun. Gavin gave a brief nod. "It won't hide me if anyone comes looking, but at least it's sheltered."

He gritted his teeth against a wave of pain as Talianna dragged him under the bushes before pulling the cloak from beneath him. The ground pressed cold against his stomach, shivers going up and down his spine before his body grew used to the difference.

Talianna swooped the tattered cloak around her shoulders, her hands pausing as she fastened it at her neck. "Are you certain you don't want me to leave this? It'd keep you warm."

"No," he insisted. "You'll need it more than I will."

A shadow crossed her face, cracking the perfect mask over her expression. "Are you sure? I could—"

"Don't." The skin across his shoulders burned and stung as he pushed himself to his elbows. "Don't try to convince me. I can't give in on this any more than you can." He nodded in the direction of the rising sun. "Follow the stream; it'll take you to the coast. When you get to your uncle, tell him what happened and ask your father to send Tristan and the others to protect you." His voice cracked. "And when you become queen, remember me."

Talianna's eyes widened, her own voice breaking behind its regal cadence. "I—I will." Before he could stop her or pull away, she dropped to a knee and kissed his forehead, the feel of her lips warm even against his burning face. Her own face was flushed as she backed up, pressing a hand to her mouth before gathering it into a fist. "I'll remember. I promise."

Gavin watched as she walked away, her footsteps gaining speed as she made her way along the riverbank. After a moment, he let his head fall to his arms with a broken gasp of relief that turned quickly into a sob. The fragrance of the flowers overhead filled his senses, forest sounds a soothing cadence of peace as another shiver wracked his body. *There could be worse places to die. I just never expected I'd be alone.*

6

WOODWIFE

Talianna hurried along the riverbank as fast as she could, focusing on getting as far away from Gavin as she could before her breaking heart could have the chance to betray her. His forehead had been warm, so warm as she'd kissed him, her royal nature deserting her for a moment of weakness before she'd forced herself to walk away.

I'm leaving him to die.

As she squirmed past a towering elm, her foot slipped, and she fell heavily into the mud. The shock and surprise combined in a heartbeat with exhaustion and grief, and a sob burst from her chest. *He was crying, too, as you left,* her treacherous heart warned her as she picked herself up. *You heard him.*

Yes, she had. Less than a hundred feet into her flight, a quiet sound had reached her ears—a cry, muffled, most likely, by Gavin to keep her from turning around.

I've heard that sound from him before. She clutched her cloak tighter and slid down the tree trunk to sit huddled at its base. *And it was my fault then, too.*

The past rushed in.

"You'll need to say goodbye, Tali."

Talianna frowned as she stood up. "Are you sure?" She gently laid her croquet mallet to the side. "Will there be time after lessons tomorrow?"

"I'm afraid not, sweet." Nursie squeezed her hand with something

that felt like an apology. "Besides, your father says you must only play with children of your own rank from now on."

"Oh…" Talianna's face grew hot, and she blinked hard against the prickling of unshed tears. Across the pile of mallets, Gavin stared wide-eyed between her and her caregiver. "Are you sure?"

"Say goodbye, my love."

Talianna didn't wait for permission but yanked her hand free from the woman's grasp and dove toward Gavin. His arms met hers, and they clung to each other for a long moment.

"I'm sorry," she said into his shoulder. "I didn't—"

"I know," he said. "I knew it would happen eventually." Gavin's brow was pinched as they drew back from each other, his lips pressed into a thin line. "Just"—he scuffed a hand across his eyes—"don't forget me, all right?"

She took a deep breath. "I won't forget you." Nursie's hand was on her shoulder, already turning her away. "I promise."

Talianna risked a glance backwards as they walked toward the garden gate. The pieces of the game lay scattered in the grass, Gavin standing amid them with his head bowed and shoulders stooped. Perhaps it was her imagination, but she could've sworn she heard a sob as the tangled rose arbor cut off her last glimpse of her best friend.

Talianna pressed a hand to her mouth, but a pained gasp still crept past her fingers at the memory of what she'd done. *I left him.* After a few days of being escorted to and from tutoring sessions, she'd slipped past her nurse and made her way to the garden. There'd been no sign of Gavin. Further questions, answered unwillingly by her servants, revealed that he, too, had been sent away—gone until the moment he'd knelt before her to swear his oath.

We'd been reunited, and I still left him. A rush of tears came to her eyes, as burningly unwelcome as they had been on that afternoon so many years before. This time, she gave them full rein, pulling her knees to her chest and pouring out the years of loneliness into the silent woods.

After a while, her sobbing slowed. Then, from out of nowhere, a voice. "Why so sad?"

Talianna jerked upright, stifling a cry. "Who's there?"

The voice chuckled as a woman came into view from behind a clump of hazel bushes. "Don't be afraid, 'tis only I." She leaned against the elm and ran a loving hand over its bark as she asked, "Why are you crying?"

Talianna wiped her eyes and took a deep breath. Even though she looked young, there was something about the woman that reminded Talianna of her mother. Perhaps it was her beech-brown hair, twisted carelessly into a braid and dangling over one shoulder. Perhaps it was the way she leaned against the tree trunk—as if she was slowly merging with the forest itself—or perhaps it was her stillness; as if time moved differently to her.

"I'm in love with my dearest friend, and I've just left him to die." Having begun, Talianna found herself unable to stop. The woman listened to the story without interruption, only shaking her head as Talianna explained Gavin's insistence on her deserting him.

By the time Talianna's words slowed into silence, the woman's gaze had sharpened. Her hand tightened on the bark of the elm tree. "You say you left him upstream?"

"Yes." Talianna twisted her hands in the edges of her cloak. "He's badly hurt. I tried to help him, but I don't know anything about injuries." Tears welled up again as she added, "And some of the bandits know he's alive. They'll be looking for him."

The woman nodded as if this was a foregone conclusion. "Yes, they're on both of your trails. You won't escape them on your own, and he certainly won't." She lifted her hand from the tree trunk with a sharp look at the canopy. "We don't have much time. Follow me. Quickly!"

Gavin drifted in and out of sleep for over an hour after Talianna's departure. At first, the shade of the elder bushes and cool earth were unbearably cold, every breeze sending uncontrollable shivers across his skin. As the sun rose higher into the heavens, the chill turned to fiery warmth, magnifying the pain in his back and shoulders a hundred times over. His attempts to inch further into the shade only succeeded in reopening a few of the worst gashes, and the dirt beneath him eventually grew sticky with blood.

Worst of all, it became harder to stay awake. Fever settled around him in a heavy, choking blanket, foggy blackness giving way to the sunlit rose garden where he and Talianna had said goodbye so many years before. Like then, she was walking away from him, her shoulders straight with what he now recognized as the first time she'd assumed her royal persona. Unlike that day, her beautiful face was filled with nothing but scorn as she looked over her shoulder.

"Father says I must only associate with those of my status. Surely you know I'm far too good for someone like you. You!" She laughed. "The *younger son* of a baron! Forget friendship; you're only worth anything as a servant."

Gavin clenched his fists, temper boiling over at the unfair accusation even as part of his mind insisted that this was merely a dream. "That's not true!" he yelled, digging his feet into the grass and sprinting in her direction. The rose bushes surrounding the garden reached out and caught him, biting into his skin as Talianna's haughty laughter turned to screaming. A stone corridor opened out in front of him, flaring torches casting pools of light among oppressive darkness.

"Gavin! Help!" Talianna screamed as a masked man dragged her around a corner. "Gavin!"

He startled awake. "Tali!"

Coherence came with the fragrance of elder blossoms and the humming of bees. He was still lying on the blood-soaked dirt, Talianna's and another woman's faces framed above him by sunlight. Somehow, he'd rolled to his side in his sleep, and Talianna was holding one of his arms. "Gavin, breathe. It's only me."

Gasping for air, he tried to sit up and collapsed in agony onto his side as the other woman reached to stop him. Full memory returned then, and he laid still. "Why are you here? I told you to leave!"

"I did leave!" she protested; her voice shot through with urgency. "I didn't get far before Melina found me. She's a healer, and she can hide both of us until you're better."

"Hide us?" he gasped. "She's one woman. What can she do against all of them? We're outmatched, Tali. You need to run!"

"Look, boy." The woodwife—Melina—looked like she was only thirty, but her voice carried the same authority as any training officer's. "I don't have to tell you that you *will* die if you remain here. Trust me, no one will find you *or* your lady." Her sun-browned face was secretive as she added, "There are protections around my home that none can pass."

"Please, Gavin," Talianna pleaded. He wasn't sure he'd ever heard such a tone in her voice as she said, "She can help us. Please."

Gavin closed his eyes against the glare of the sun, which had now slanted far enough to shine fully under the elder thicket. "I—" A ragged sigh escaped his lips. "I'm in no position to argue. Just please," he let his eyes open enough to glare at Melina. "Talianna is worth more to me than anything else, including my own life. You have to keep her safe at all costs."

"Yes, yes." The woman's voice was impatient and brisk. "I swear it, Sir Knight." There was a swish of fabric and a clatter of wood. "Now, be still and let me help you."

"Where are we?"

Talianna jumped as Gavin spoke. Hearing his voice, roughened and pained as it was, sent a wash of relief over her limbs. "You're awake!"

Melina spoke from beside a small hearth as she ladled steaming water into a bowl. Beside her, herbs hung on the whitewashed earthen wall above a polished wood sideboard. "This is my home. I tend to the people who live in these woods and who know where to find me."

"But the bandits don't?" Talianna asked, her voice catching in her throat with sudden fear. "If they find us—"

"They won't. You're safe here, but your knight is still badly hurt." Melina came to crouch and look Gavin in the face. "Sir Knight, if you are going to survive this, I need to clean your wounds." She held a finger in front of his face. "It will hurt."

Gavin gave an exhausted blink. "I understand." A flash of fire went through his eyes. "Does Talianna need to be here?"

Talianna crossed her arms as the woodwife gave her a questioning look. "I'm *not* leaving."

"So be it." Melina tossed her a drying cloth. "Go wash."

Over the next hour, Talianna came to respect the older woman immensely as she painstakingly cleaned and dressed the wounds that the bandits had left on Gavin's back and shoulders. Talianna's heart cracked a little more with each flinch, each gasp of pain from him as dirt and blood were sponged away and dying skin cleared.

All this time, I'd been measuring men by their social status and education, when all along the worthiest man I knew was standing a few feet behind me. She renewed her grasp on Gavin's hand as Melina went to switch dirtied water for fresh. *I can't believe I was so blind all those years.*

After what seemed like ages, the many cuts and swellings were clean, covered in healing balm, and wrapped in layers of light bandages. Talianna fell asleep leaning against the whitewashed wall beside Gavin, his hand still clasped in hers. She woke to find darkness outside the shuttered window, and a smell of food coming from the other room. Gavin still slept, his blond hair damp and darkened with sweat when Talianna laid her hand on his head.

Careful not to disturb him, Talianna poked her head into the other room. Melina stood at a solid table near the hearth, mixing greens in a wooden bowl. "Ah, you're awake. I just came back from checking my traps."

Talianna wrapped her arms around herself. Even with summer's warmth, the earthen house was chilly. "Don't the bandits bother you?"

The woodwife shook her head, and something feral stirred in the depths of her eyes. "They won't try me. Not if they don't want the trees to swallow them alive."

Talianna's breath caught in her throat. When she could speak, her voice had gone thin and squeaky. "Are you a witch?"

"I am not." Melina said firmly. "But you're forgiven for think-ing it. My grandmother was a guardian of the forest—a dryad, I suppose." She flicked her gaze toward the ceiling, where the ridges of tree roots crisscrossed the whitewashed ceiling. "They respect me, and no one comes near me or my home unless they allow it. That's how I knew you and your knight were being hunted."

"The…trees." Talianna pressed a hand to her mouth. "When the bandits were about to kill Gavin, something shook the ground and scared them. Did—" She let her hand drop. "Were the trees watching?"

"Mm-hmm." Melina stood on tiptoes to retrieve a basket from a shelf above the table. "The old blood still runs in the deeper parts of your kingdom, Princess. You'd do well to remember that."

Talianna glanced out the door of the kitchen. Gavin still slept, his bandaged back gently rising and falling under the thin blan-ket. *She's helped us so far. I have to trust her.* "Will we be all right here?" She nodded at the door. "Will *he* be all right?"

Melina took a handful of mushrooms from the basket, her movements slowing along with her words. "I've done what I can, and my skill is good. But you felt it as well as I did—he's gone feverish, and there's not much I can do if infection sets in. You've known each other for many years?"

"Yes." The simple admission didn't seem adequate, so she added, "Since childhood." *When duty pulled us apart.* "And this isn't the first time he's saved me. I don't know what I would do without him."

"Well, do all of us a favor and pray that he pulls through this." Melina swung a kettle over the fire. "There's only so much that my medicine can do."

That night, Talianna slept on a blanket next to Gavin's cot. She woke a few times to hear him sob in his sleep. In her dreams, the trees whispered secrets through the ground, their creaky voices murmuring, *No one else has been worthy. No one until now.*

GAVIN DIDN'T KNOW HOW long he drifted between waking and sleeping before finally waking to find Talianna holding his hand.

"You've been asleep for three days," she told him, relief lightening her expression. "Well, mostly asleep. Do you remember anything?"

"Only nightmares," he said. "And I think I heard your voice a few times."

She smiled at that. "Melina says your fever's gone. You should be on the mend faster, now that you're not burning up from the inside."

While Talianna's words proved true, it was still another day before Gavin was able to sit unaided. After that, his strength returned quickly. There was something in Melina's care that brought restoration faster than he'd thought possible, until he could walk around the tiny house without his muscles shaking. As the week passed, it became achingly apparent that something had shifted in Talianna's attitude toward him. She rarely met his eyes, and their conversations were marked by tension; as if she was remembering something he had forgotten.

One afternoon, the tension finally broke. They were sitting outside Melina's home, shielded from the setting sun by the leaves of the trees over the house. The woodwife was nowhere to be found, gone on one of her many expeditions through the forest to collect food and check on her traps. Gavin hadn't been certain what he thought about her relationship with the trees, but the proof of her loyalty could easily be felt in his rapidly healing injuries. Besides, there had always been stories told about these woods.

Talianna made a frustrated noise beside him as she examined the rip she was mending in her cloak. The sound was so unlike her usual way of approaching difficulty, and her face so preoccupied with something beyond the simple task, that Gavin couldn't keep silent any longer. "Tali? What's the matter?"

She shook her head. "Nothing."

Gavin reached over and put a hand on her knee, moving carefully to keep the healing skin under his bandages from ripping open. "It's not nothing. You're acting different."

Talianna sighed. "I know. I'm sorry." She set the sewing down and, after a moment's hesitation, put her hand over his. "With everything that happened to you and what you said when I left, I don't know how I should act anymore."

"With what I said… What did I say?" Gavin pulled his hand away, his mind spinning with terrifying possibilities. *I was so feverish, I don't remember. I think she kissed me, but that* has *to be a dream. Did I say something foolish? What's she going to think? What's her father going to think?* He pressed his lips together. "I don't remember what I said. It's all a blurry mess. Tali, what did I say?"

Talianna looked down at the sewing in her lap. "You said you were replaceable." A tear rolled down her nose. "You had no idea you'd survive, but you did everything you could to keep me safe even at the risk of your own life." Her shoulders shook under a shuddering breath. "You sacrificed for me, bled for me, and you *still* called yourself replaceable." Her head flew up, brown eyes turned to gold in the setting sun. "Don't you understand? How can my life mean that much and yours so little?"

"No, Tali," Gavin stammered. *How is she getting this so wrong? Can't she see how precious she is?* "I'd sworn to protect you years ago, even before giving my oath to your father. Together or apart, you've *always* been the one I'd choose above all else!"

Her eyes widened. "What are you talking about?"

"Just after that day when you had to say goodbye," he hastened to explain. "My father sent me away as well; to page training." The memory of those days thrummed through his mind.

"Every family commits at least one of their sons to service. And I need your brother here."

Gavin took the letter as his father passed it across the desk. He fought to keep the quiver out of his voice, the paper crumpling in his fist as he stood as tall as he could. "Yes, Father."

"Don't worry; it won't be all bad. You'll train with the realm's best, and when you're through, you'll be a knight." Lord Andel stepped from behind the desk to hold Gavin by the shoulders and look him squarely in the eye. "I'm proud of you, son. It's a great honor to be able to serve."

Gavin nodded, ducking his head as his father released him. Riding away from the palace the next day, the memory of Talianna's straight shoulders and fierce expression caught his mind. She'd looked so small as she walked away, like the weight of the nation already pressed against her.

"She'll become queen someday," he whispered to himself, drawing his own shoulders straight. "And when she does, she'll need someone to watch out for her. I can do that, even if it means we won't ever be together again."

"I swore that day that I'd protect you with everything I had," he finished. "You're brilliant, Talianna, and not just the way everyone likes to think." His voice caught as fierce longing flooded her eyes, bright and beautiful as the warmth speeding through his chest. "You're as brilliant as the sun, Tali," he whispered. "And I've never been able to keep you out of my heart."

Before he could stop her, she hugged him. Gavin squeezed his eyes shut at the sudden pain in his back and concentrated instead on how soft her hair was against his face.

"You've hidden it all this time," she said as she sat back. The expression on her face was a perfect picture of contentment, so far removed from the perfect mask of court life that Gavin wondered for a moment if he were still feverish. "Did you ever wonder if I might feel the same way?"

"I never dared to hope," he confessed, nerves making his stomach tense. "There's such a gap between our stations, and I'm leagues below the type of man you need at your side."

"Father's only stipulation was that I choose someone worthy." Talianna flushed pink. "The rest I added because I assumed everyone expected it of me." She shook her head, the color deepening in her cheeks. "I can't believe it took something like this to break me of the thought that worthiness was only measured in status and power. I'm so sorry."

"It's all anyone's told you since you were eight," Gavin said. Warmth stirred in his chest, relief dissolving his nerves as he added, "I think I forgive you."

He'd dreamed of kissing her for years, but this was not how he had imagined it would happen. Leaning forward, careful of bandaging, he gently kissed her on the lips. Talianna froze for a moment before leaning into him, gold-touched eyes fluttering closed as her hand found his. Their interlaced fingers tightened for one, two heartbeats before she drew away with a dazzling smile. The sunlight turned the leaves golden, and for a few minutes, he was able to forget the danger.

7

SEASIDE

AFTER THE GREEN AND gold dimness within the forest, the sunlight glimmering off the sea was almost too bright for Talianna's eyes. Yet there the sea was, stretching out before her in depths as uncharted and hostile as the forest had seemed only a short while before.

"I've spoken with them," Melina had told her and Gavin almost ten days previous, one hand on the trunk of an oak tree as if she were merely translating the words of her timber kindred. "They'll ensure your path is swift and secure as you make your way to safety. Though, I think they may have done that even without being asked. They like you, Your Highness." The woodwife's eyes had shimmered green for a moment as she added thoughtfully, "Perhaps the old blood runs closer to your family line than you thought. If you ever have need, they'll answer to your call."

As nerve-wracking as the journey through the remainder of the forest had been, it was still strange to leave its green depths for the sunlit plains between it and the sea. Fife Corbel sprawled along the edge of the ocean, its coastal grasslands patchworked with hay meadows and livestock grazing fields. While not extremely wealthy, Talianna's uncle had nonetheless managed to build his fife's economy up enough to support a small harbor town some miles away from his castle's walls.

Almost four weeks after leaving the palace, Talianna and Gavin presented themselves in the courtyard outside the manor house of Fife Corbel. Neither had been able to bathe since leaving the woods, Gavin was unshaven, and their clothes were dirty from the road. However, the man at the gate went to fetch his master with only a few backward glances as they stood wearily on the threshold.

"I think they may not have known we'd look like—" Talianna paused, wondering exactly what her uncle's staff might have been told.

"Like peasants?" Gavin finished with a mischievous look in her direction.

"Yes!" she laughed. "You barely look like a knight, and I *certainly* don't look like a princess."

He laughed as well, but the amusement died in his face almost as quickly as it had begun. "Whoever is in charge didn't communicate well. We're later than expected; enough that the caravan with our things probably beat us here. They ought to have been watching for us."

Talianna clasped her hands nervously and looked up at the castle as it rose above the walls. It was built more for comfort than defense, with high, arched windows along the main building's upper levels. The courtyard beyond the gate housed a sprawling garden, where summertime flowers brightened the stone outbuildings, fountains, and practice court. Despite the concern and worry shaking her stomach, Talianna had to smile at the memories of summers spent within these very walls, before studies and her mother's illness had forced travel to cease. "I spent a lot of summers here."

Gavin nodded. "Your father mentioned that." His eyes narrowed as he looked first at the building, then the grassy slopes surrounding the walls. "I know this is far enough that anyone who wants to harm you will have difficulty finding you, but I'll still feel safer once you're *inside* the walls."

"Talianna! Holy Lord of Light, my dear girl; we've been worried sick about you!" Talianna's smile froze on her face as her aunt's unmistakable voice resounded across the courtyard. Trailed by the guardsman who'd gone to fetch her, the lady of the fife bustled across the space between manor house and gate to seize Talianna in a bosomy hug. Half-smothered in perfume and taffeta, Talianna only half noticed as Gavin slipped from her side to resume his traditional position several feet behind her. *That's right. No matter what happened in the woods, our situation hasn't changed.*

The thought barely sank in as her aunt released her and kept talking. "Your things arrived a few days ago, and we've put them in the tower rooms. I didn't even know when to expect you; the letter from your father said there were complicating factors surrounding your departure." She stopped and looked appraisingly at Talianna. "You're a mess, darling. What on earth happened?"

"We had some difficulties on the road, Your Grace," Gavin interrupted from behind Talianna. She had to hide a relieved smile as he took a firm step forward to come between her and her aunt. "I have reason to believe that the princess's situation here could already have been compromised. Her Highness requires a bath and clean clothing, and I need to speak with Lord Corbel at once to make preparations for her safety."

Lady Corbel practically jumped. "Oh, of course. Silly me." She grabbed Talianna's hand and waved them both forward, exclaiming, "This way, both of you. Milord isn't here now; he and the boys are finishing up some business at the port, but he'll be back the day after tomorrow." She led them into the main house before catching the attention of several servants. "You there, fetch hot water to Her Royal Highness's rooms at once."

THEY WERE SHOWN TO a suite of rooms on one of the upper floors of the main building. Gavin was pleased to see that his and Talianna's accommodations were on the same floor, his room adjoining her sitting room by a hidden door. Sure enough, their belongings had arrived already, and his single chest stood in the corner of his room. He quickly shaved and washed up in the basin near the door and put on a set of his own clothes. Digging in his chest, he retrieved his second-best wrist knife—the unmarked one he'd meant to take with them before their hectic departure from the palace. Tightening the straps around his forearm, he shook his head at his own foolishness. *That's another time one of your failures put her in danger.*

A more rational part of his mind chimed in as he folded a scarf to cushion the small of his back, where new scars crisscrossed healing skin. *The bandit leader made things very clear; someone hired them to ambush us. The odds were against us from the moment we left the palace.* He carefully belted his own sword over his tunic and checked that it was still in good condition. It felt so good, so right, to have the weapon he was most familiar with riding at his hip where it belonged.

Talianna was still in her room when he came out, admiring the way the door closed seamlessly behind him. He paced the floor of the small sitting room, examining the windows and doors. The windows were small, not matching the large-paned arches that graced the side of the building facing the courtyard. He tried the catch on one, and it swung open to allow air and light but not much else. The doors, likewise, were sturdy and banded with metal to stop even the most determined intruder. Whatever his reservations about their situation, their host did know something about ensuring Talianna's rooms were secure.

He wandered over to the writing desk and selected a pen and paper. Writing carefully to avoid smudging the ink, he started penning a letter to the king's council to request a squad of men to be sent to Fife Corbel. Halfway through his description of their journey, however, he stopped.

I'm not sure who leaked news of our departure. Gavin rested his chin in his hand, frowning at the paper as if it could provide him the answers he needed. *Only a handful of people knew Talianna was leaving the palace, and most of them hold high positions within the guard, the council, or both.* He swept the half-written letter from the desk and into the newly laid fire before starting on another, this one addressed directly to Lord Kelmar. *I have to make sure she's not left vulnerable here, and of anyone, he's the one I trust the most.*

He was sealing the envelope shut when Talianna's door opened and she came out, wearing one of her own dresses and with her hair gleaming in a long braid.

"It feels so good to be clean again, and in my own clothes." She tipped her head toward him, a frown creasing the space between her eyes. "Didn't you bathe?"

"I will later," he said. "I wanted to get a head start on some things first." He slipped the letter into his belt. "Did your aunt say the Earl was gone?"

"Him and my cousins both. I think they'll be back soon. Why?"

"I have a letter to send, and I prefer to send it secretly." He gave her a sheepish smile. "After what happened, I'm suspicious of everyone."

Talianna's expression sobered. "I understand. Now more than I ever did." Her gaze flickered between him and the door as one of the maids went out into the hallway with an armful of laundry. When she next spoke, her voice had dropped to a plaintive whisper. "Gavin, what are we going to tell them? About"—she raised a hand helplessly between them—"about this?"

"I'm not sure." Gavin paused, wishing more sunlight could make its way into this small-windowed space. The forest hadn't been kind to them, but it *had* filled Talianna with liveliness unlike anything he'd seen inside a stone building. "I know you'd been wanting to write to your father as soon as you could, but Tali, I'm afraid that whoever paid the bandits is someone very, very close to your father's confidence." He frowned and ran through the very short list of possibilities in his head. "There are only a few people who knew we were taking the forest road, but I'm not sure who hired the bandits to kill us."

Talianna glanced at the door before stepping closer to him and gently wrapping her arms around his torso. Her hair smelled of rosemary, braid still damp as she laid her head against his shoulder. "I'd hoped this would be a safer place."

"It will be, if I have anything to say about it." He held her close for a moment before letting her go. *Keep your wits about you. If you let down your guard now, it could spell disaster for both of you.* "I'd just sleep better if I knew who it was that wanted you dead."

SEVERAL DAYS LATER, GAVIN followed Talianna down the stairs to the dining room for a formal family dinner. True to Lady Corbel's predictions, Talianna's uncle had returned from business a day or two previous, and had wasted no time in ensuring his niece was made comfortable. Even with his prompt attention to Talianna, Gavin was unimpressed. He'd met the earl at court several times and was irritated to find that his previous assessment of the queen's brother as 'snobbish and condescending' was still the case. *I think I understand why the king never offered him a position at court. At least he's always been kind to Talianna.*

The sounds of cheerful talk and laughter filled Gavin's ears as he and Talianna stepped into the comfortably appointed dining room. Taking his customary place by the wall alongside the other family servants, he watched and listened with amusement as Talianna greeted her aunt, uncle, and her cousins. *You'd think they'd been apart for decades,* he thought as Lady Corbel kissed Talianna's cheek enthusiastically, *and not just for the afternoon.*

His amusement quickly died as Talianna's older cousin Roderick helped her into her seat with a practiced bow. He'd forgotten until Talianna's reminder that the children of the household spanned two decades—two older sons that Lady Corbel had borne to her first husband, and a pair of much younger daughters from her union with Talianna's uncle.

"Roderick and Brendan aren't really my cousins," Talianna had explained earlier that week. "Aunt Adeline's first husband died a few years ago, and she remarried. It's just easier to call them that, after my uncle adopted Roderick as his heir."

Well bred, well spoken, accomplished and *wealthy. Son—or at least heir—of an earl.* Gavin assessed the dark-haired older brother with a practiced eye before turning his gaze to the younger of the two men. They were even within a few years of the princess's age. *If it weren't for the familial ties, either would have been an acceptable marriage match.*

He pushed the thoughts away as dinner began, Talianna's laugh sending a shimmer through his heart and bringing to mind recollections of their time together at Melina's home. Freed from royal constraints of public life and cheered by the discovery of love, their conversations had been long, sweet, and deep as he recovered his strength.

But it can't be like that here, he reminded himself as Lord Corbel impatiently snapped his fingers at one of the menservants. *Not around other nobles. Not around anyone who won't understand. And certainly not until I make sure that she'll be safe.*

After dinner, the family retired to a library adjoining the dining room to talk and catch up. Gavin followed, taking an unobtrusive seat at Talianna's insistence. While the family chatted, he let his thoughts turn once more to the problem of reinforcements. The letter to Lord Kelmar had left via courier the day prior to Lord Corbel's return, but he knew better than to expect a response of any kind in less than a few weeks. *Assuming they decide it's worth the risk of breaking secrecy.*

Deep in thought, he hadn't noticed the drift in conversation from court gossip to the circumstances surrounding his and Talianna's departure from the palace until Roderick commented, "It was quite the ordeal for both of you to get here, I understand." Talianna's older cousin had gotten up from his seat and was leaning against one of the bookshelves, his eyes hardly leaving

Talianna as he said, "Mother mentioned that you met with some trouble, but she didn't say what kind."

Gavin couldn't stop his posture from stiffening. He'd told Lord Corbel the whole story in their meeting but hadn't considered what the rest of the family had heard.

Talianna answered for him. "There were complications, yes. Though, I can't speak of all of them." She gave Roderick a dazzling smile that Gavin suspected was calculated to distract more than charm. "Security, you know. We were planning on leaving soon after the festival, but then one night—" In short sentences that left more unsaid that said, Talianna summarized their harrowing journey through the forest. The rest of the family listened with rapt attention, Roderick giving Gavin a cursory approving glance as Talianna explained that he'd been injured in protecting her from the bandits. Even with Talianna handling the tale, Gavin couldn't help a quiet exhale of relief as she finished with, "Had Sir Gavin not acted as he did, neither of us would be enjoying your hospitality now."

"I'm glad he was able to ensure your safety." Lord Corbel said. He cast a more than halfway dismissive glance at Gavin. "I'm certain that you won't have any more difficulties now that you've arrived, dear niece. My men are very dedicated to our family, and any intruders will be hard pressed to reach you with their expertise surrounding you."

Talianna nodded serenely, but Gavin noticed her jaw tightening. "I'm looking forward to the summer activities, though I'll rest a bit easier once Sir Gavin has had the opportunity to strategize." She tipped her head to the side, a flicker of cunning sliding through her cheerful mask. "Can we determine a time for him to meet the men he'll be commanding?"

Gavin had to hide a smile. *He might not see me as an equal, but he'll be hard pressed to refuse his niece.*

He'd gauged Lord Corbel's reaction appropriately. With a few more minutes of conversation, plans were laid for Talianna and Gavin to meet the men-at-arms who'd be assigned to Talianna's personal guard for the duration of her stay in Fife Corbel.

"Perhaps you'd also like to meet on the practice grounds?" Roderick suggested. "It's been a while since I was able to spar with a new opponent." He thumped his younger brother's shoulder gently, earning a grey-eyed glare. "Brendan here is good, but it's not often we get the chance to face off against another knight."

Gavin smiled, ignoring the worried look Talianna flashed him. "I'd welcome it. It's been a while for me as well." *I need to get back into practice.* He frowned slightly as the conversation moved to other topics. *We got out of the woods alive, but there's no telling what will happen once our enemies find out where we are.*

8

CONTEMPT

THE NEXT MORNING, GAVIN met with the men chosen to protect Talianna and assigned them a schedule of guard duty. He wasn't extremely impressed with them, but he reasoned this was a symptom of having worked with the best men the kingdom could offer. More concerning was Lord Corbel's attitude. Talianna's uncle had insisted on attending the security briefing, and what ought to have been a focused planning session devolved into a struggle to maintain his authority over the men-at-arms. Gavin left the meeting fuming and uncertain if any of the plans he'd laid would even be followed in the event of an emergency.

Later that afternoon, Talianna and her maids joined him on his walk to the practice courts at the edge of the castle grounds. The two women weren't anywhere close to the nobility that had marked her previous companions, but Gavin couldn't deny that they knew a thing or two about taking care of their royal mistress. Someone—either the maids or Talianna herself—had selected a blue dress with gold accents for her to wear today, and he wondered if she knew how pretty it made her look as they walked across the grounds.

"Are you certain about this?" she asked, the levity in her voice not completely hiding her worry.

"I'm not worried. I'll be careful." He flexed his shoulders under his shirt, new scar tissue pulling as it stretched. "Besides, I need to hit *something*, and if your uncle overrides my orders one more time, it's going to be him."

Talianna's mouth pressed into a straight, stern line. "I'm sorry."

"It's all right." The words came out a little more harshly than he meant them to. "I'm used to it."

He and the brothers saluted each other as they met in the practice courts, Talianna and her maids taking seats in the shade of a nearby grape arbor. A few of the other men-at-arms were already practicing, and the clatter of practice swords soothed his frustration faster than any kind words would have.

"I know we're nobility and all, but don't go easy on us, all right?" Roderick said as they squared up for their first match. "We could use the practice."

"If you insist." Gavin hefted his practice sword. Its balance wasn't quite what he preferred, but the weighted wood still felt good in his hand. "So long as you promise you won't go easy on me."

Three matches in, Gavin was beginning to wish he'd exaggerated his confidence less. His muscles were getting shaky, and his ribs hurt from where Brendan had gotten a lucky hit against him. Worse, the confidence lent by sparring—and winning—had waned as Talianna's aunt and uncle came to join her in the shade. They'd kept to alternately chatting with Talianna and cheering for their sons, but Gavin couldn't shake the feeling that he was being assessed and found lacking by Lord Corbel. *Does he suspect something about Talianna and I? Is that why he's been so difficult?*

Roderick wiped sweat off his forehead. "One more?"

Gavin glanced over his shoulder at the group under the grape arbor. Talianna's maids had left, and she was happily talking with her aunt, but Lord Corbel gave him a measuring, condescending glance. A chill ran up Gavin's spine. "I think we'd better make this one the last."

"All right." Roderick raised an eyebrow, challenge filling his voice as he assumed a 'ready' position. "Nothing left behind for this one?"

Gavin settled his shoulders. *Remember, he's not his father. Don't hit him too hard.* "Nothing. Give me your best."

Their matches had started slowly up to this point, each combatant testing the defenses of his opponent before attacking. This time, there was no preamble. Gavin circled away from Roderick, pausing only a heartbeat before lunging. Roderick swore and jumped back a pace as Gavin's sword crashed against his.

"Careful!" Brendan shouted from the sideline.

The group under the grape arbor seemed to have noticed that this bout was fiercer than the previous one. As his and Roderick's swords met once more, Gavin saw Talianna lean forwards with concern. *She's going to think I'm being stupid. I shouldn't worry her.* A glance at Lord Corbel's unimpressed face wiped the momentary hesitation from his mind. He lowered his sword and stepped back a fraction, tempting Roderick to make a foolish move. Roderick took the bait, swinging forwards at Gavin's unprotected arm. Jumping backwards and stepping to the side, Gavin leveled his sword point at the back of his opponent's neck. "Yield."

"Don't let him beat you so easily!" Lord Corbel shouted, the words echoing across the arena. "Show him what you're made of!"

Gavin didn't think he was missing the anger that sped through Roderick's face as the other man turned to smash aside his blade. Just like that, the fight was joined again; backwards and forwards across the dusty sparring ring until Gavin's chest was heaving and his arms burning with exertion. He swung at Roderick's side, but his opponent managed to dodge aside at the last moment. Suddenly, his vision went white as something solid hit him across the shoulders. Crumpling into a heap on the ground, Gavin let go of his weapon as Roderick angled his sword at his throat.

"Yield!"

It took an agonizing long moment before Gavin found his voice again. When he could finally speak, it was as if through a mouthful of dust. "I yield." He blinked slowly as the pain shooting through his shoulders subsided. "You've been holding back."

Roderick offered him a hand up, the anger that had clouded his face replaced with cautious pride and respect. "So have you. You had me fairly, the first time." He flicked a gaze toward the grape arbor, where Lord Corbel's face had flushed with pride. "I'm sorry about him."

"I'm used to it." It was easier to say to Roderick than it had been to Talianna. "Some people only see my rank, not my title." He bent to pick up his practice sword. *And being used to it is my own lie.*

"I understand," Roderick said. He nodded toward the others. "Let's reassure your lady that you're all right."

The pain in Gavin's shoulder hadn't lessened by the time he stepped into the shade. Talianna had her hands on her hips, her beautiful face darkened with worry as Lord and Lady Corbel moved to congratulate their son. "Are you all right? Are you hurt?"

He shook his head, plucking at the ties on his jacket and shaking it free. "I'm all right, but I think—" Gritting his teeth against the pain, he dragged his shirt over his head. A damp patch slithered past his face, an unmistakable metallic tang warning him of what had occurred.

"Gavin—" Talianna's voice was hushed. "You're bleeding."

Something burned behind his right shoulder, and he caught a glimpse of fresh blood as he turned his head. One of the lash marks had split open. Before he could say anything, Talianna had pulled a handkerchief out and was pressing it into his skin. "Don't move," she murmured. "It's not that bad."

He looked up uncomfortably to realize that the others around the practice yard had gone quiet. In the shadow of the vines, Gavin could only imagine what they might—or might not—be able to see. He clutched his discarded shirt with both hands, the sudden warmth of shame sweeping over him.

"I—" Lady Corbel's voice had gone thin and shaky. "You mentioned there were injuries, but—"

"What happened?" Lord Corbel demanded, surprise overtaking the sneer in his voice. "What did he do to deserve this?"

Gavin's fists closed into tight knots around the fabric of his shirt. *Only slaves or criminals have scars like this. From now on, everyone will assume the worst.*

He was about to respond, and not politely, when Talianna stepped in front of him. Her spine was perfectly straight and her voice composed as she explained, "The bandits knew who they were looking for. Sir Gavin refused to turn me over, and they did this. They assumed he was dead, and if we hadn't come across a woodwife who helped us, he would have been." Her voice rang with authority as she added, "I owe my life to him." The words settled like early frost over the practice arena as she turned to him. "Sir Knight, I'd appreciate it if you'd escort me back to my rooms."

Weariness sank into his bones as he got up. "Yes, Milady." He shook out the crumpled, bloodstained shirt and pulled it on over the open cut. It was better being in pain than being the object of everyone's stares as he followed Talianna across the courtyard to the house. Behind him, he could hear Roderick's and Lord Corbel's voices, both intense with the heat of an argument. The defense heartened him, but nothing could quite undo the shame still burning his face and gnawing at his heart.

She'll have to defend me like this as long as I'm guarding her. I love her, but I can't expose her to that kind of contempt.

NOT EVEN THE COLD depths of her royal persona could temper the frustration churning through Talianna's stomach. She threw the front door open and made for the stairs. Her skirts caught with each step until she grabbed them up out of the reach of her shoes. Gavin trailed her like a silent shadow up the stairs. He hadn't spoken since she'd demanded to leave the practice courts, and it was a surprise when he finally said her name.

"Tali," His hand landed on her elbow. "What's the matter?"

She dropped her skirt and turned to face him, politeness vanishing in peculiar fury. "Him!" She began stomping up the last flight of steps toward her room. "Did you see the way he looked at you? *Talked* about you? Like you were only some foolish commoner!"

"I noticed." An edge had crept through Gavin's voice, at odds with the stoic politeness he usually displayed around other nobles. "He doesn't seem to care much for me. At least your cousins don't seem to mind."

"Exactly! They don't care, because why would they? As a

knight, you outrank them. You've seen battle and they haven't. But to my uncle—" Talianna's foot caught in her skirt, and she stumbled on one of the last steps.

As quick as thought, Gavin's hand was at her back, his other arm under her elbow to steady her. "To your uncle, I'm nothing more than a servant," he said quietly, as if he hadn't just saved her from falling. The arm around her shoulders tightened in a brief embrace before letting her go. "Don't worry about it. I'm not bothered."

They climbed the last few steps in silence. As they reached the door to her suite, the pressure against Talianna's heart built until something cracked inside. "Wait."

Gavin stopped behind her. "What is it?"

"Marguerite and Gabrielle will be inside. And I have something to say." She craned her neck to look down the hallway. For the moment, they were alone. "Gavin, I can't let this continue. What happened in the forest—it changed everything for me. I know we have to carry on acting like nothing ever happened, but I can't. I just can't."

For a moment, fierce hope flared in his eyes before disappearing under some invisible shroud. "Tali, don't," Gavin whispered. "We can't. Not here. Not around other nobles, not around anyone who won't understand." He looked at the floor, his hand tightening at his side and desperation pitching his voice. "Maybe not ever. I'm so far below you in rank; no one would accept it. And just now—that type of talk—you'd hear it for the rest of your life; people always whispering behind your back—"

"Our backs," she interrupted. "I meant what I said, in the woods. Father left the choice of my husband up to me, and while there were several good candidates, they all lacked one very important thing." She swallowed hard, remembering every ball, hunting party, and festival where the princess had blinded everyone to the girl yearning to be seen. "You looked past the princess and saw me. Just me. And you thought that girl was worth dying for." She caught her breath and pronounced, "I want to spend the rest of my life with you, and not just with you following one step behind me."

She hadn't realized she was crying until Gavin reached up to brush a tear from her cheek. "You really want this?"

She nodded. "It's the only thing I can choose for myself, and you're the only man worth choosing."

He took a deep breath, frustration and hope warring across his face. "Then," his voice came out hushed and helpless. "What would you have me do?"

"Ask." She smiled. "Just ask."

Gavin's eyes closed, brow creasing as some inner battle raged where she could neither see nor hear. Finally, his eyes opened to reveal green touched with gold as brilliant as the sunlight through forest leaves. He took a deep breath and said, "Tali, I've loved you for longer than I can remember. I know I'm below your birth, and you deserve someone who is more your equal. But there's no one else I can think of who I'd rather spend my life with." Her heart skipped a beat as he whispered, "Will you marry me?"

He'd kissed her in the forest, surrounded in a cascade of golden light. Now, in the darkness of the hallway and surrounded by the weight of duty, expectations, and contempt, she kissed him. Fabric rustled as he pulled her closer, the scars he'd earned saving her life pressing against her hands through the softness of his shirt. The warmth that normally guarded her back surrounded her as she whispered against his chest, "Of course I will."

9

BETRAYAL

TALIANNA WROTE TO HER parents the following day.

"I don't like it, Tali," Gavin warned. They were briefly alone in her sitting room as her maid Gabrielle ran an errand downstairs, and Talianna stood in the comforting circle of his arms. She rested her head against his shoulder with a frustrated sigh as he reminded her, "We still don't know who paid the bandits to kill you, and I'm afraid your letters to your father may not remain as private as any of us would like."

"They need to know, even if Mother doesn't understand." She pulled her face away from his shoulder to look up at him. "Father made things clear that he expected me to return from this summer with a choice in mind, so things could be announced after my birthday in the fall."

"So soon?" His arms tightened around her a fraction, the sheath of his wrist knife pressing against her shoulder blade with the reassurance that his strength could turn from comfort to protection in a heartbeat. "I thought—"

"Father's health isn't as good as he makes it appear," she confessed. "I think he's getting worried. He once told me that I'd have as long as I needed to decide, but lately he's been pressing me more and more each time the subject comes up. If I had to guess, I think he's nervous that he'll pass without my future being settled."

Gavin let her go, one hand going up to run through his blond hair in a helpless gesture. "I knew, but—"

"He hides it well," she said, stepping back from him as her maid entered the room with a tray of tea. "I understand it's a risk, but this type of information can't stay between us."

He nodded, a pained look crossing his face. "Send it, then."

WEEKS PASSED. GAVIN AND Talianna did their best to behave as normally as possible, though Talianna soon suspected that her lady's maids had found out about their engagement. Although not of noble birth or court training, Marguerite and Gabrielle had caught on quickly to the duties of attending a princess—including noticing when their mistress needed privacy. The remainder of the family didn't seem to notice anything amiss between Talianna and Gavin, though Talianna assumed they were still too awkward with Gavin to notice anything else.

As the days slipped past, everyone fell into a peaceful routine. Still, between socializing with her aunt and younger cousins, Gavin's weapons practice with Roderick and Brendan, and the occasional horseback ride outside the castle walls, Talianna noted the passage of time with growing impatience.

"It's odd," she said one morning. Her maids perched on one of the settees in her sitting room and focused on needlework while she and Gavin read. "I sent that letter to Father quite a while ago, and I still haven't heard anything from him." She gave Gavin a significant look. "You know the one. I thought for sure he'd reply quickly, once he read it."

"That *is* odd." Gavin closed his book and frowned at the fire-place. "I also expected reinforcements from your personal guard to arrive, or at least a message that they were on their way."

The sudden silence in the room rang more fiercely in Talianna's ears than the noise of any crowded ballroom. She looked over at the older of the two conspicuously silent maids. "Marguerite, is something wrong?"

The woman didn't look up from her embroidery, giving an emphatic shake of her head. Gabrielle, the younger maid, set down her sewing and whispered something in her ear. With a frustrated look at her workfellow, Marguerite said quietly, "His Grace has been stopping your letters from leaving, Milady."

"What!"

The maids exchanged uncomfortable looks. "He gave us orders to give him any letters you sent," Marguerite said. "He told us it was for your protection."

Gavin groaned. "That *does* seem like something he'd do, and never mind telling us."

Talianna stood with a rush of skirts. "I think we need to talk to him." Lord Corbel's attitude toward Gavin had remained annoying as ever since the accident at sparring practice, and it didn't surprise her that he'd taken extra security measures without bothering to inform them. "Coming?"

Gavin picked up his sword from where it had leaned against his chair. "Coming."

Leaving her rooms, they passed the men-at-arms who stood on either side of the door and went down the stairs to Lord Corbel's study. Her uncle seemed taken aback when she explained her findings. "I'm sorry, my dear," he said, coming out from behind his desk to take Talianna's hand. She swallowed distaste at the feel of his clammy fingers as he said, "Given how perilous your situation was when you arrived, I thought it best that correspondence between the fife and the palace be temporarily halted until things settled. Though, here." Lord Corbel released her to rummage in an ornate box. He finally withdrew an envelope, sealed with the crimson and gold that marked her father's private correspondence. "This arrived just yesterday for you."

"And you didn't think to give it to me right then?" Talianna assumed the tone she typically used with minor courtiers—the tone that placed the title of 'Her Royal Highness' at the forefront of her voice. "Milord, regardless of your concerns, my correspondence with my father must take priority. There are urgent matters that need discussing, no matter the risks involved."

"Of course; I'm sorry for the oversight." Lord Corbel handed her the letter. "I'll ensure that there aren't any more occurrences like this. Unless you had anything else, Milady?"

"No, that was all," Talianna said. "I'm grateful we were able to clear up this misunderstanding." She glanced at Gavin, who'd taken up his usual spot behind her. "Gavin? Did you have anything you needed to bring up?"

"Actually, yes." He folded his arms. "I must also protest, Milord. I'm uncomfortable knowing that such an important aspect of Her Royal Highness's security was dealt with without being brought to my attention." One eyebrow raised, a challenge if she'd ever seen one. "Going forward, I'd appreciate any such measures being discussed with me *before* being implemented."

Lord Corbel gave an exasperated sigh. "Yes, yes, of course." He waved a dismissive hand in Gavin's direction as he ushered them out the door. "You have my word. Now please, I must prepare for a meeting with my steward. If you'll excuse me?"

As the study door closed behind them, Talianna gave an annoyed huff. "Father would have never sent us here if he'd known how obnoxious my uncle was going to be." She shook her head. "He wasn't like this when I was a child, I promise you."

"I believe you. Your father isn't a fool." Gavin nodded at the letter in her hands. "I *am* grateful that he wrote, at least."

"Me, too." She frowned at the dimly lit hall. "It's too dark to read down here. Come on."

GAVIN FOLLOWED HER UP the stairs. The windows were large and graceful on the second level of the house, casting sunlight in regular rectangles on the carpeted corridor floor. Talianna broke the crimson seal and pulled several sheets of paper forth, eyes scanning each in turn. The sunbeams behind her edged her dark hair with light even as her face was thrown into shadow—a shadow that deepened the longer she read. When she looked up, her face had frozen into a formal, composed mask. "We might be too late."

Fear hammered at his heart. "What are you talking about?"

Talianna waved the papers. "M-my father. Before I left, I got fed up with his constant worrying over my marriage, and I told him he was free to make the decision for me if he thought he could choose better." She thrust the letter at him, her voice stretching dangerously close to a wail. "He always refused—he said he'd never take something from me that I deserved for myself. But now, he says that given how dangerous our journey was, he has no choice but to decide on my behalf. Look!"

Gavin stared, uncomprehending, at the words on the paper in his hand.

…harrowing journey leaves me no other option…confirm the line of succession before your return and lend stability to the realm…Roderick of Corbel, a man worthy of your time and attention.

It was instinct to reach out and pull Talianna close, holding her as tightly as he had the afternoon when they'd said goodbye as children. *We were so close to happiness.* He buried his face in the top of Talianna's head, the softness of her hair hearkening back to the moment when she'd hugged him in the forest. *At least, now, it doesn't hurt to hug her.*

At that, some part of his mind caught on the memory of new scars burning under bandages—and arrested his swirling thoughts. "Tali," he said carefully, "How did your father find out what our journey here was like?"

"I told him, remember?" she said, the thin disbelief in her voice layered under the kind of composure that said she was trying hard not to cry. "In the letter I wrote."

"The letter that was never sent." He released her to step back and look into her eyes. "It never made it to him; how did he know what happened?"

She shook her head. "It doesn't matter. He's made his choice; you saw the seal just like I did."

"I saw the seal," he answered as gently as he could. "Just—check again, please. Are you *absolutely certain* it was him who wrote this?"

He turned to look out the window as Talianna examined the letter once more. *I don't know which I hope for; to be right or to be wrong.*

A quick intake of breath sounded beside him. "This isn't Father's handwriting." Talianna looked up at him, her face painted with confusion. "I can't believe I didn't notice it before. Gavin, he *never* uses a scribe for personal letters. And—" She flipped between pages with a new urgency. "He always uses my nickname, no matter how serious the matter is. There's no mention of it here. I—" Her eyes darted at the stairs as a chambermaid walked past with a pitcher. "Something isn't right."

Gavin took her arm and drew her close enough to where no one could possibly overhear. "Someone else close to your father had to have sent this; someone who could get access to his seal. Someone who knew you were here but also knew what the journey was like."

"My uncle may have said something…"

"Perhaps, but if that were the case, why wouldn't your father have sent more men to guard you?" A warning hum had begun in the back of his head. "Your uncle may be stupid, but your father isn't. Tali, there's too much here that doesn't match."

A shadow passed over Talianna's face, as if a reflection of her royal persona had been cast over the woman inside. "You sent a letter of your own to the palace to request reinforcements, before my uncle arrived home and stopped our correspondence," she said, her voice low and filled with tension. "Who'd you address it to?"

"Lord Kelmar." Something grim yawned in the pit of Gavin's stomach, his muscles tightening as if to absorb an unexpected blow. "Something felt off about his story the night we left, but I trusted him enough to obey his orders." He caught his breath as another thought struck him. "The orders that were also sealed in your father's name. Lord Kelmar may have had access to your father's seal. And he's the only one, other than those here, who would have heard what happened in the forest."

A spark flashed through Talianna's eyes, and they narrowed. "The bandits had knowledge about the specifics of how we were traveling. You said they knew exactly who they were looking for."

He nodded helplessly. "There were only a few people who knew the circumstances of our departure, but Lord Kelmar knew the most. My only question is, how much of this does your uncle know? Is he conspiring with them?"

Talianna wrapped her arms around her torso. "I don't know! I would have said never, but with the way he's acted, I don't know any more." Her eyes locked onto Gavin's. "This was supposed to be a safe place."

"You're right." Certainty settled in his mind. "And if I have anything to say about it, it will be." He fished under his sleeve and drew his wrist knife, pressing the hilt into Talianna's hand. "Get to your room. Stay there."

Talianna nodded, icy strength filling her gaze. "Where are you going?"

"I'm going to find proof." He pointed to the end of the hall. "Go!"

She went, glancing back before vanishing around the corner. Gavin made for the other stairwell, moving as quietly as he could along the polished steps. "I hope Milord Earl actually *did* need to consult with his steward," he muttered, barely more than a whispered threat. "Otherwise, this conversation will be much more direct than anyone wants."

Luck favored him. Lord Corbel's study stood empty, the inkwell capped and pens set aside. With a rapid glance at the door, Gavin slipped behind the desk and began efficiently rummaging through stacks of documents. After long minutes, he found what he was looking for. In a box buried deep in one of the drawers, Gavin uncovered a document written in a familiar hand and sealed with a foreign signet. It was the work of a moment to read the contents of the entire missive, his heart thumping harder with each passing word.

"Holy Lord of Light," he exclaimed under his breath, lowering the document with a pair of sentences burned into his mind.

With the princess well in our grasp, all that will remain is for an accident to befall the king. With His Majesty's failing health, no one will question his sudden death.

"It's worse than I thought," he gasped, stuffing the paper into his tunic. The sound of the drawer closing came mirrored, as the study door opened with such force that it rebounded against the wall. Two men-at-arms rushed in, weapons drawn and at Gavin's throat before he could free his own sword.

"Sir Gavin!" Lord Corbel's aristocratic voice was surprisingly strong as he strode into the room with another guardsman at his heels. "Why am I unsurprised to find you here, meddling in matters far above your station?"

Gavin's heart hammered in his chest. "Why?" he demanded, certain the paper tucked into his tunic was crackling loudly enough for everyone to hear. "How could you plot against them like this? They're your family!"

Lord Corbel shook his head condescendingly. "My brother-in-law has never appreciated true leadership. And with him out of the way, Talianna will need guidance. She may be my sister's daughter, but she's still a woman. She needs power surrounding her—men of true breeding and noble quality to guide her steps." The corner of his mouth twisted into a sneer. "It's something her father should've seen years ago."

"I don't care what power you think you deserve," Gavin snapped. "Plotting against His Majesty will always be treason. And Talianna doesn't need your help. She's brilliant without anyone at her side."

Lord Corbel smirked, the taunting in his voice coming straight from Gavin's nightmares. "That's exactly the type of thing a servant with everything to gain *would* say." He snapped his fingers at the guardsmen. "Get him out of here."

The men-at-arms lowered their swords only long enough to yank Gavin's arms behind him. He twisted and shoved as they dragged him out the door, shouting as loudly as he could before one of them slammed an elbow into the side of his head. Everything went dark.

10

ULTIMATUM

TALIANNA PACED HER BEDROOM, measuring the footsteps until she knew by heart exactly how many of her paces it took to cross in each direction. *Wait for me,* Gavin had said, but as the hours slipped past, dread began growing in the pit of her stomach.

Something is wrong. She bit the inside of her lip, worrying at the tangled knot of thoughts and emotion as if it were a logistics problem set by one of her tutors. *Lord Kelmar. The bandits. Father's letter. Uncle's strange behavior.*

Eventually, her emotions settled, one unexpected thought rising to the surface of her mind as raised voices sounded in her sitting room. *Prepare for battle, Talianna.*

She opened her bedroom door to find Gabrielle standing with her back to it, her hands outstretched and pleading. "I told you, Milord, Her Highness isn't well! She—"

"I'm here, Gabrielle," Talianna said, laying a gentle hand on the girl's shoulder. She locked eyes with her uncle, whose face was approaching the angry red of midseason strawberries. "I'm feeling much better. It's all right; you can go."

Gabrielle gave her a stricken look before obeying, skirting the guardsmen and disappearing into the hall. Talianna took the moment of silence in the wake of the door closing to compose herself. "I wasn't expecting to see you until later this evening, Uncle," she said as she stepped farther into the room. "Is everything all right? Where's Gavin?"

Her uncle gave a short laugh. "Oh, him? He was found rummaging through my study."

Talianna's stomach clenched at the words, but she kept her face as smooth as possible. "That doesn't sound like him," she said. "It's possible there's been some kind of misunderstanding. Where is he now?"

"I've detained him. He won't be disturbing our conversation, if that's what you're concerned with." Lord Corbel nodded toward the paper she still clutched to her bodice. "I see you've read your father's letter."

Talianna glanced down. Her book still lay on the side table, the ribbon she'd used to mark her place a bright spot of color in a room devoid of sunlight. "I have," she answered cautiously. "I assume you received a similar one?"

"I did." Her uncle sat down without invitation, withdrawing a scroll case from his belt. "He included these." Papers crackled as he removed them from the case, their embossed edges curling across the table and hiding her book from view. "It's all arranged, and requires only your signature to complete."

Talianna tilted her head, a chill spreading through her at the sight of her father's official seal. *I need to play for time. Gavin wouldn't have been imprisoned unless he'd found something he wasn't meant to see.* "What exactly has been arranged? What is this?"

"A contract of betrothal to Roderick. Also, documents placing me in the position of advisor to your Majesty, once you take the throne."

Talianna paged through the documents, her concern deepening with each new revelation. *Betrothal contract, reorganization orders for my finances, the beginnings of a new household structure.*

If I go through with this, I'm reducing myself to a pawn in the hands of my advisors. Deep inside, she had to offer grudging respect to whomever had devised the scheme. *This is much more sophisticated than merely attempting to stab me.* Finally, she looked up, simmering anger buried deep under ironclad composure. "I see here that you would also have control of my household once I am married."

"Acting in your best interest, of course." Lord Corbel crossed one knee over the other. "A queen will require a trusted advisor who can handle the daily affairs of her household. And who better than your own father-in-law?" He gently shifted the documents from her hands, pressing her fingers between his. "Tali, I know it can't have been easy, laboring under the weight of this choice for years. It's unfair to place the responsibility of the realm's future entirely on your shoulders. I'm only grateful that your father was finally able to lift the burden from you."

For a moment, he sounded like the affectionate uncle of her childhood. Tears unexpectedly welled from her eyes, and she bowed her head. *Rest and freedom, at last. An end to all the speculation. Someone else to share the load.*

It would be so easy, if only I wanted it like this. Talianna took a deep breath, the pressure of her uncle's pudgy hand against hers bringing to mind every stifling moment when she'd sacrificed the girl inside for the sake of the princess. Her hand curled into a fist as she pulled it free from his grasp.

"You have no understanding of what royal pressure feels like," she whispered. "And God help me, you never will." She raised her head, authority swelling in her voice. "My father gave me his word that my choice would remain my own. If this is truly his wish for me, then I need to consider carefully before I give any kind of meaningful answer. Even if I agreed to marry Roderick, there are certain things that will require alteration." She pinned her uncle with a clear-eyed stare. "As things stand, I'm unwilling to place so much responsibility in the hands of someone who's behaved so discourteously to me and demeaned those who I value most."

Her uncle's face flushed. "You mean Sir Gavin? Talianna, he's a *servant.*"

"He's not just a servant, Uncle," she said. "He's nobility, even if his bloodline isn't written in gold. He's earned the position he holds, and my father trusts him with my life." She nodded toward the door. "Thank you for delivering the documents. Please leave—*now*—so I can think this over."

She didn't think Lord Corbel was used to being ordered about in his own house. He strode to the door, hands clenched into fists. On the threshold, however, he turned to face her once more. "If what you said reflects your heart, then I'd caution you to think carefully of your next actions." He narrowed his eyes. "Remember, it is only you that is irreplaceable to the realm. Sir Gavin is of little consequence."

Talianna felt as if someone had poured a trickle of ice down her back. She shot to her feet, matching him stare for stare to cover her sudden fear. "Leave my rooms this instant," she hissed.

A triumphant light shone through the earl's eyes. "As you command, Milady." The door slammed behind him.

Talianna sank into her chair with shivers running up and down her limbs. The unexpected threat had completely disarmed her fearless persona, and her stomach clenched in knots at the realization of the powerful weapon she'd handed her uncle. "Oh, Gavin." She pressed a hand to her mouth. "What have I done?"

BLACKNESS.

What in—Gavin's hands flew to his face. No blood or pain met his fingertips, and he breathed a relieved sigh. Blinking hard, he peered into the darkness until, finally, a sliver of light registered on his consciousness. He was lying on a chilly stone floor, the light a crack beneath the door of the room. Slowly getting to his knees, then his feet, he groped around until he was certain of his surroundings—a storeroom of some kind, most likely in the basement of House Corbel. The darkness was less disorienting with his eyes closed, so he shut them again and felt his way back to the door.

Sitting with his back against the wall, he pulled his knees up and wrapped his arms around them to conserve body heat. The movement made the paper in his tunic crinkle, and he pulled it free with a grim chuckle. The guardsmen had taken his sword and other weapons, but the hastily tucked paper had somehow escaped their notice. *They'll regret that, once their master finds out it's missing.*

He smoothed the paper across his leg before running his fingers down its surface until they reached the textured wax seal. *Lord Kelmar's handwriting; I'd recognize it anywhere. But a foreign seal—a Treluthian seal. And they're not only after Talianna, they're after the king as well. If His Majesty dies and Talianna takes the throne while in their control, we'll be at the mercy of our enemies.*

He sighed and let his head fall back against the wall, half-remembered visions of the border posting lurking past the edges of his mind. *His Majesty's staved off open war through diplomacy and subterfuge time and time again, but campaigns are never fought on just one battlefield. Us coming here was meant to avoid complications, but I didn't expect our enemies to be one step ahead of us.*

A thought occurred to him, so ironic despite his situation that he had to laugh. *This ploy of controlling Talianna instead of outright killing her really is their best one yet. I almost wonder if they're glad she survived the forest.*

The paper folded small enough to be tucked between his sock and his calf, in the spot where a boot knife ought to have rested. With the incriminating document hidden, he got to his feet and began pacing the small space. *Talianna can't agree to this. I don't think she will, anyway—even without knowing about the threat to her father, she's smart enough to recognize a terrible decision when she sees one. But more than that, we need to get word to the king—or warn him ourselves.*

Gavin halted his pacing, eyes now adjusted enough to the darkness to notice the shift in light at the bottom of the door as someone approached. The door opened in a squeal of ungreased hinges, admitting a blinding wave of light broken by the shape of a guardsman. Gavin flung himself toward the opening, smashing the man's head against the wall and bolting into the corridor beyond.

Torchlight pierced his vision, as blinding and disorienting as the darkness had been. Voices rang through the corridor, some-one yelling, "Stop him!"

A hand caught at his shoulder, and he twisted wildly, his shirt-sleeve tearing. He punched the person holding him, and his fist ached as the blow connected. His assailant staggered backwards with a gasp, the sound familiar enough that he pulled his next punch long enough to recognize Talianna's cousin Roderick. "You!"

The hesitation was all it took. A spear haft thudded across the back of his head, and he staggered and fell. Voices swirled around him, mixing with the clank and rattling of metal on stone. He felt himself dragged, and something cold snapping closed on his wrist before the voices subsided. Eventually, the world tipped right side up once more. He was still in the storeroom—now illuminated by lantern light—with his right wrist manacled by a chain fixed into the wall. Roderick leaned against the opposite wall, his gaze equal parts concerned and wary as he said, "Welcome back. We need to talk."

Gavin's head spun as he dragged himself into a sitting position. "Why are you here, traitor?"

"The earl sent me." Roderick winced and put a hand to his collarbone where Gavin had punched him. "He wanted me to make sure you were well secured, and now, I think I understand why. At least you didn't break anything." He stopped and shook his head, voice growing exasperated. "Will you stop glaring at me? I promise, I'm not here to bother you."

"Really?" Gavin didn't bother hiding the sarcasm in his voice as he rubbed the back of his head. The dizziness was lessening, but a splitting headache had begun. "You did a really fine job of showing it."

Roderick held his hands up, his dark eyes flashing. "I'm not the one who attacked the first person through the door! And if I hadn't let them knock you out, they'd have kept hurting you." He looked away, his voice lowering in something that sounded like shame. "It's the earl's orders. He wants Talianna to sign over her freedom in exchange for your safety."

Pain welled in Gavin's heart. *I knew we'd been too obvious. How can I have been this stupid?* "I hope for her sake that she doesn't," he answered bitterly. "And you'd better be warned; it'll take a lot more than your father's bloodthirsty guardsmen to break me."

"I know." Roderick shifted his weight from side to side. "Look, I see how much you care about Talianna. It's obvious in how you've put yourself in danger to protect her." He raised an eyebrow. "That kind of disregard for your own safety goes beyond an oath of duty."

Gavin looked up in surprise. There was respect in the other man's eyes. "And?"

"My father's actions, whether successful or not, are going to ruin my life. If he succeeds, I end up a puppet king. If he fails, I'll suffer along with him for my part in his schemes." Roderick fixed his gaze on the floor. "I respect my cousin, and I do feel that she and I could make a good partnership, but I can see that I'm never going to win her heart."

Gavin forgot all about his headache. The chain around his wrist clanked as he got to his feet, using the wall for support before standing on his own. "Help us, then."

"How?" Roderick shook his head. "You don't know what I know. You don't know the—" His voice dropped, and he glanced at the door. "You don't know who he has behind him. Or what they'd do to my family if I did anything other than play along." He passed a hand over his face, desperation roughening his voice. "My mother, my brother—Holy Lord of Light, my *sisters*—they're trapped in this as certainly as I am."

"Trapped or not, we need to do something," Gavin argued. His stomach clenched at the panicked look on the other man's face, but he forced himself to keep his mind on the only thing that mattered. "Where is Talianna now?"

Roderick frowned. "Her rooms. She's not letting anyone in, and she threw my father out when he went to try and speak with her."

"That does sound like something she'd do." Gavin glanced at the door, uncertain if there was anyone outside who might overhear. "You know there's more to this conspiracy than just Talianna's future. Our entire country will crumble if your father and his allies get into power."

"You're right. That's why I'm here." Roderick sighed. "If it weren't for who he's working with, I'd have stayed out of this and done whatever I needed to in order to assure my mother and siblings' safety." His hand balled into a fist. "He's not really my father anyway. Mother only married him after my and Brendan's *real* father got killed in a border skirmish with Treluthian outriders."

Gavin took a sharp breath and steadied himself against the wall, its bulk solid against his hand as visions of several years ago flashed through his mind in a blur of red. "Your father was there?"

"He was there. Mother knew marrying Lord Corbel would ensure our security, but I don't think she ever expected he'd join forces with the men who were responsible for her first husband's death." Roderick's face had been stony, as unmoving as Talianna's face when she was at her most regal. Now, Gavin recognized the growing desperation in the other man's eyes, and it brought to mind a piece of wisdom from his training master. *Never back an enemy into a corner with no way of escape,* the man had warned. *You never know what he might be willing to try.*

"If my stepfather's masters take power, there'll be violence. No matter what they think, they won't find this country willing to fall into their power easily. My family's story will be played out hundreds of times over." Roderick lifted his head, light burning fiercely in his eyes. "Helping you is the only way I'll have any hope of protecting my family *and* retaining my honor. I don't know how we can stop them, but—" He took a single step toward Gavin and put out a hand. "Allies?"

Gavin eyed him for a long moment. Finally, the chain rattled as he extended his own hand. "All right."

11

ALLIANCE

"I DON'T BELIEVE YOU," Talianna said flatly as she stared at Roderick across her sitting room. It'd been hours since she'd banished her uncle from her suite, and her tiny windows now opened only onto darkness. Her shoulders felt tight, and her head ached as if she'd been bearing the weight of her ceremonial coronet the whole day. *And in a sense, I have.*

Roderick crossed his arms. He'd kept his distance since being shown in by the men-at-arms outside the door, barely stepping into the circle of light cast by the fire. "I've told you everything I can. I don't want my mother and sisters to suffer if Father finds out what I've done."

Some of Talianna's hostility drained away, replaced by exhaustion. "I can't fault that." She sank into a chair. The door to Gavin's room stood open beside the fireplace, his absence at her back sending a hollow, lost feeling through her chest. "How long have you known about the plot against my father?"

"Not until today. Father didn't see fit to mention it until after he'd arrested Sir Gavin." His voice dropped to an ashamed whisper, the echoes of a frightened child coming through it as he said, "He told me to go downstairs with the guards and hurt him enough to make you change your mind."

Talianna's head shot up. "And you *listened?*" She stormed across the room and yanked open the door. "Get out. I can't believe I thought for even a moment that you'd help me. You're as bad as he is!"

Something she couldn't name flashed through Roderick's dark eyes. "Talianna, stop." In one step, he was at the door, pushing her aside and closing it with such force that the frame rattled.

"Don't touch me!" she spat, drawing back a hand to slap him with all her strength. "Leave me alone!"

Roderick caught her wrist before the blow could land. "I *didn't hurt him*, Talianna. I swear." He released her and took a step away, holding open hands in front of him. "I did what I could to keep him safe."

Talianna drew instinctively back. Roderick was barely an inch or two taller than her, but in the darkness beyond the firelight, he seemed so much bigger. *I couldn't get past him even if I had a weapon.* "Then tell me the truth," her voice cracked. "Do *you* want this?"

"Do I—" Roderick's jaw dropped. "No!" He stepped farther away from the door, the firelight casting a glow over the side of his face. "I only want my family to be safe. I can't stand the way my father looks at my sisters—the girls *he* was responsible for bringing into the world." The glow spread over his face as he kept retreating. "He thinks they're nothing, the same as he thinks Sir Gavin is nothing. He can't be trusted with power, Talianna. And neither can the men he's working with."

Talianna took a deep breath. "Then who are they?" She pointed a warning finger at him. "You say you're on my side, so prove it. Who is directing your father in this lunacy?"

For a moment, she thought Roderick wasn't going to answer her. Then, he dug in his pocket and flipped a gold coin into the air. It flashed in the firelight, landing with a heavy thud on the rug. Even in the dim lighting, Talianna could make out the double-headed wolf of Treluthia.

"Them?" she whispered. "*That's* who's behind this?" She bent to pick up the coin. It felt every bit as heavy in her hand as it had sounded when falling to the floor.

"Father gave that to me when he explained the rest of his plan this afternoon." Roderick had stepped closer to the fire, its light edging his green tunic with gold. "Along with about ten others. He must think I'm as driven by greed as he is."

Talianna closed her hand on the foreign coin, its edges digging into her palm. Something dangerous had begun stirring in her chest at the sight of the crest, as determined as the light she'd seen in Gavin and Roderick's eyes each time they sparred. "He'll regret that decision soon," she vowed. The fire warmed her face as she crossed to stand in front of it, returning the coin to her cousin. "If we're going to warn my father, we need to move quickly. Can you get us horses and supplies?"

"Yes, easily. Especially with how much gold Father just tossed my direction. But my mother, my sisters." Roderick turned the coin over in his hand, a frown stamped on his face. "I can't leave them. You're going to have to escape on your own, and you know what happened the last time—"

Talianna took a deep breath, the popping of an ember falling on her ears like a whip crack. "I know. But last time, our enemies were ahead of us." She dared to smile at her cousin, the light playing across his form reminiscent of the sun shining through leaves. "This time, we'll be ahead of them."

Several days passed, as filled with tension as an archer's bowstring. For Talianna, the hours had become a deadly game of chess against her uncle, as she drew upon every ounce of diplomacy and strategy she possessed to avoid signing the documents that still lay upon her sitting room table. After the first day, she'd been confined to her room save for closely supervised walks in the grounds with Roderick.

"If I'm to spend the rest of my life with him by my side," she'd insisted. "I have to be given the opportunity to speak with him one on one. No matter what my father says, I *cannot* agree to marry someone I've had so little time with."

Her uncle had reluctantly agreed, and this afternoon saw her and Roderick walking between the grape arbors of House Corbel. The heat of summer lay heavy against Talianna's skin, and the scent of flowers and horses filled her senses as they passed the stables. "You *were* able to secure horses?" she murmured, quiet enough that the servants tending the gardens would be unlikely to hear.

"I did." Roderick stopped and directed her attention to one of the paddocks, where two horses—one bay, the other blue roan—were being exercised by a groom. "Those two, there."

Talianna nodded approvingly. "Thank you. I'm not the best judge, but I think they're beautiful."

She thought Roderick was about to say something else as they rounded the paddock, but his eyes flicked to something behind her, and his posture stiffened. Talianna turned with sudden fear clutching at her heart to see her uncle approaching them, flanked by two men-at-arms.

"Talianna," Roderick said from behind her, his voice low and urgent. "Do you trust me?"

Adrenaline shot through her veins, cold composure seizing her limbs. She lifted her chin. "I have to."

"Good." He stepped past her, posture and voice both shifting to something more confident as he addressed Lord Corbel. "Father, thank you for joining us."

"My pleasure. You did what we'd arranged?"

Talianna thought a shudder passed through Roderick's shoulders as he nodded. "I did. Perhaps you'd like to escort Her Highness?"

Sickening dread crept through Talianna's stomach as her uncle came to take her arm. "Of course. Milady, please join us." It wasn't phrased as a request.

"What's going on?" she asked as they entered one of the service corridors of the main house. "We'd barely started our walk, and—"

"Please, spare me," Lord Corbel said, releasing her arm as, ahead of them, Roderick struck flint to steel. Torchlight bloomed in the opening of a stairwell. "I'm a patient man, Talianna, but these delaying tactics are getting tiresome."

Talianna squinted in the dimness at the bottom of the stairs. The doors opening off the corridor looked like storerooms or wine cellars—*Or cells.* Her heart started pounding. *Gavin. He's here.* She turned to her uncle. "Why are we here?"

"I warned you that your servant meant nothing. So far, you seem determined not to listen." Her uncle rounded a corner into a passageway lined with storerooms. Two guards stood at the end of the corridor, Roderick already striding to join them.

Talianna stopped and pressed a hand to her mouth. One of the men-at-arms put a hand to her shoulder, urging her forward as her voice came out shrilly. "What did you do?"

"Only what I promised would happen if you continued to be stubborn. Open it," Lord Corbel ordered.

Roderick pulled a set of keys from his belt without meeting Talianna's furious gaze. The door squealed on ungreased hinges as he opened it. "Here."

Talianna wrenched her shoulder free and ran to the door. Her heart sank at the sight of Gavin, sprawled on the floor unconscious with his face bloodied. "Gavin!"

Roderick caught her with an arm around the ribcage as she pushed past him. "I'm sorry, Talianna."

"Let go of me! Let go!" she shrieked, all sense of princessly composure gone as she rounded on her uncle. "How could you do this!?"

"This doesn't have to happen, Talianna," Lord Corbel said from the corridor. "It can stop at any time." His expression hardened. "You can stop it at any time." He gave a curt nod to Roderick. "See if you can talk some reason into her, then take her back to her rooms. I'll be in my study."

As her uncle's footsteps retreated, Talianna managed to elbow Roderick in the side. "I trusted you," she hissed as he doubled over with a groan. "You beast!"

A familiar voice cut through her rage. "Tali, stop."

She looked up, wide-eyed. Gavin was sitting up, blood staining his sleeve as he wiped it away from an otherwise unmarked face. He returned her shocked expression with a reassuring smile. "It's all right."

Talianna shoved Roderick away and fell on her knees next to Gavin. She wrapped her arms around him, fingers clutching his shirt in a fierce embrace. "You're all right?"

"I'm all right," he reassured her, gently drawing her back before brushing an errant curl from her forehead. "I'm not hurt, Tali. It was a trick."

"But the blood—"

"Not mine," Gavin said. He looked up at Roderick, still standing in the doorway. "I think it was a chicken?"

"A duck," Roderick said. "And it was more difficult to get *that* than it was to get the horses."

The door screeched closed, leaving the three of them alone in the tiny room. "I'm sorry, Talianna," Roderick said as he came to kneel alongside her, eyes cautious as if he expected her to hit him again. "We needed something to happen that would result in you barring everyone from your rooms, and I couldn't risk your reaction being anything other than real."

Talianna sat back on her heels. "This was planned?" She shot Gavin a look that was meant to be fierce but dissolved into a smile. "You've been working together?"

"We came to an understanding." The chain trailing from his wrist clanked as he wrapped his hand around hers. "This part was Roderick's idea, though. We weren't sure how else to take your uncle's attention off you."

"I'm not sure how long it'll buy you," Roderick added. "Hopefully, enough for you both to get out of the fife without being pursued."

Urgency stirred, tempered by the reassuring warmth of Gavin at her side. "We're leaving soon, then?"

Both men nodded, but it was Gavin who answered. "Tonight."

THE SUN HAD LONG sunk below the horizon when Talianna slipped down the stairs behind Roderick. The brush of her cloak against the stairs, coupled with the feel of her boots against her feet, was so eerily reminiscent of the last time she'd fled under cover of darkness that she found her nerves coiling into tight knots as the sally port in the outside wall came into view. Gavin waited just beyond, holding the reins of the two horses she'd seen earlier that day. He met Roderick with a brief handclasp before catching her in a strong, one-armed hug and pressing a kiss into her temple. "No trouble getting out of the house?"

She shook her head and pulled her hood over the scarf she'd wrapped around her hair. "Not yet."

"You need to hurry," Roderick warned from the sally port. "The guards aren't the most attentive to this side of the house, but there's always the chance that one of them might decide to be thorough for once." He passed Talianna a satchel. "That's everything I was able to collect from Father's study. It should have the details a magistrate will need to bring him and his allies to justice. Just—" His features were dark in the shadows under the wall, but she could hear the uncertainty in his voice. "Remember my family when you decide my fate."

Regret stung Talianna's heart. Any magistrate would undoubtedly view Roderick's involvement with his father's plans as damning and treasonous—a fact he certainly knew as well as she did. "I'll try."

"Protocol may not allow her to speak on your behalf, but I can," Gavin said beside her. "You were handed the chance to take power for yourself and chose not to. That'll mean something in the right ears. I'll do whatever I can to keep you out of prison and away from the headsman."

"Thank you," Roderick said, taking a step backwards with a cautious glance at the top of the walls. "You'd better go. I'll stall my father as long as I can. You'll be all right traveling through the forest?"

Talianna accepted Gavin's boost into the saddle. "We'll be all right." She peered into the darkness, envisioning the green depths of the woods. "There are things in there that not even your father's masters could have predicted, and we didn't leave without allies."

THEY RODE HARD THROUGH the night and into the next day. Spurred on by the need to put distance between themselves and Fife Corbel, Gavin kept their pace as fast as he dared until the rolling plains melted into the fringe of the woods. Dismounting alongside a stream, he tipped his head back and looked up at the green canopy as the horses drank. Talianna slipped from her horse as well, coming over and leaning against him. Her shoulders hitched with sobs as she buried her face in his tunic front. "I don't want to be back here."

Gavin closed his arms around Talianna and held her tight, his own chest shuddering with suppressed tears. "I know," he whispered. "I know."

"I had to be so *royal* with Roderick," she said against his chest. "I had to be certain of everything, and there was no one to *see* me."

He drew back from their embrace and gently cupped the side of her face in his hand. "I see you, my sunlight. I always have.

And we're going to be all right." He gave the treetops a glance. "Though, it would be extremely helpful if your hunch proves accurate."

Talianna nodded, drawing a deep breath as she stepped away from him. Gavin laid a cautious hand to his sword hilt as she walked between the trees in the little clearing, her fingertips trailing the bark of each. Finally, she gave him a sheepish smile, so far removed from her regal composure that he had to smile back. "I don't know what I'm supposed to do."

Gavin shrugged. "That woodwife said they liked you. And you *did* get their attention when I was in danger." He looked up at the canopy of leaves, intertwined branches blocking out the sky in a lacy labyrinth of foliage. The sounds of the forest filled his ears, thus far carrying no hint of danger. *I can't believe I'm suggesting she talk to the trees.* "Try," he finally said. "We never know what could happen."

"All right." Talianna crossed to the foot of an oak tree. With a deep breath, she splayed both hands across the craggy bark.

The leaf-filtered sunlight deepened, and Gavin could have sworn a tremor passed through the ground. For an instant, the brown and gold in Talianna's eyes became touched with green, the bizarre light fading like a forgotten dream almost as soon as Gavin noticed it. "Anything?" he asked, half afraid of the answer.

Talianna frowned. "I think so." She raised a hand to her brow, voice going hushed. "I—I think they heard me. It was like hearing someone I'd known my entire life."

Gavin nodded. "Old blood, hm? Perhaps the stories knew what they were talking about."

"Maybe. Though we should probably still travel quickly. We have a long way to go."

12

NOBILITY

THE BLESSING OF THE trees followed them through the forest for the next several days—revealing itself in leaves rustling counter to the breeze, a path unexpectedly smooth, and passage so swift that Gavin could hardly believe it to be true. Talianna alternated between cheerful and pensive, occasionally staring into the green depths with a look on her face that said she herself barely believed the favor that followed them. Sooner than either of them expected, they were nearing the edge of the forest. The canopy had thinned, and Gavin began to see the towers and crenelations of the palace in the distance as he and Talianna came over a rise, leading their horses behind them with slow steps.

"Home," Talianna said beside him.

He looked over to see a wistful smile crossing her face. "Didn't think you'd miss it as much as you have?"

She brushed a hand through the leaves of a weeping willow. "So much about me is different now. I hadn't expected it would still feel the same, but somehow, it's still home." The wistfulness faded from her face as she looked down the path, calculating intelligence taking its place as she asked, "Are you ready?"

Gavin nodded, turning to tighten the straps holding their bedrolls to his saddle. "We need to get inside and find Tristan. I don't think it'll be safe to make any moves on Lord Kelmar until we've gathered reinforcements." He had to hide a wince as he faced forward once more, the scars across his back still tight and unaccustomed to the twisting movement. "I know I'm not supposed to admit to being afraid, but this number of unknown factors is frightening. We know their plan is for your father to suffer an accident, but we don't know when or where. And I'm not sure how to get close to your father to warn him without putting us both in danger."

Talianna's face pinched in a frown. "The servants' corridors, to start with. Though, now that I think about it—" She looked up at the sky, which was becoming more visible through the tops of the thinning trees. "What day is it?"

Gavin shook his head. "I have no idea." He counted back the days in his head from when they'd left Fife Corbel. "I think it's coming near the end of the month."

"You're sure?"

"As sure as I can be," he said. "We left at the beginning of summer, and it's getting close to Midsummer now..." A chill went up his spine at the thought. By the look on Talianna's face, she had come to the same conclusion. "If I were going to stage a fatal accident in order to create chaos in a kingdom—"

"They're going to make their move soon," Talianna finished for him. She eyed the distant palace with the same type of grim determination he usually associated with soldiers facing the enemy. "We may not have much time."

THEY SKIRTED THE EDGE of the woods until they reached the gate through which they'd departed so many weeks before. Once there, Talianna pulled her hood up to cover her face while Gavin talked in undertones with the guards. From the cadence of their conversation, and the body language that slowly shifted from suspicion to respect, she gathered that they recognized him—and that he'd managed to gain their trust.

Maybe it's for the best that others hear about the outside threats. Then, if we fail, maybe some will suspect that everything isn't as it should be. The thought of failure sent creeping fingers of dread up and down her spine, and she shivered despite the heat of the summer sun. *We're doing all we can, but what if it's still not enough? I've studied and prepared to the best of my ability, but I'm not ready to lead a country to war.*

She was shaken from her teeming thoughts by Gavin's return from his conversation with the gate guards. "Let's get out of sight."

He led her toward one of the stables, where they left the horses and their belongings in an empty stall. Talianna made sure to grab the satchel of documents that Roderick had given them before following Gavin into one of the service corridors that paralleled the main hallway of the palace. Servants scurried everywhere, most so intent on their work that they barely took a second look at either her or Gavin as he led the way toward the royal family's rooms.

Catching up with him at a corridor juncture, she whispered, "No one's recognized me."

He gave her a fleeting smile. "You're not supposed to be here, and you're wearing commoner's clothes. The servants are too busy, and the nobles won't see you at all."

Her hand went up to the scarf she'd hidden her hair in. Comparing herself to the servants bustling past, she estimated that she resembled a scullery maid or lower-class maidservant. "That's something my tutors never covered."

"It's easy to be invisible when all anyone sees is your job," Gavin said. Belatedly, she remembered all her uncle's jabs as his voice hardened. "No one thinks a servant's life is worth much, anyway."

"I'm sorry."

"It's all right." He shook his head, but she caught the flash of a lie in his eyes as he turned away. "Let's get to your rooms. There's a good chance that some of the guard will still be posted there, and they can gather the others while we warn your father."

She nodded, resting a hand on the satchel at her side. The documents and foreign coins weren't heavy, but her shoulder still felt weighed down with the urgency of the situation. They hurried up the twisting stairs that led to her room, the lantern-lit stairwell echoing with their footsteps before Gavin pushed open the servants' entrance to the sitting room.

Immediately, his shoulders stiffened, and his hand went to his sword hilt. "Tali, run!"

She had barely enough time for a fleeting glance into the room before her vision caught a glimpse of armed men and the glitter of drawing steel. Then, instinct took over, and she sprinted, pell-mell, down the staircase and back into the labyrinth of servants' corridors.

Gavin wasn't sure who was more surprised; himself or the men-at-arms around Lord Kelmar. He took in the contents of the room—barred door, nondescript clothes, and more than one person with noble bearing—in the heartbeat before hands went to weapons and voices raised in surprise.

"Tali, run!" He kicked the door shut on the echoes of Talianna's footsteps, put his back to it, and drew his sword.

THE DOOR AT THE bottom of the stairwell burst open as Talianna stumbled into the servants' corridor on the second floor. She slammed it behind her and ran down the corridor, not slowing her steps until she'd turned two corners and gone down another flight of stairs. Once surrounded by the steam and clamor of kitchen, scullery, and laundry, she paused at a corner to compose herself. Her hand tightened around the strap of the satchel. *Gavin's bought me a few minutes, but it won't last. I need to get help.*

THERE'S TOO MANY OF them. Gavin gasped as one of the guardsmen's swords traced a stinging line along his arm. He stepped back as far as he could, his boot catching on the outflung arm of a downed man. Balance lost for a split second, he regained his footing only to find his grip on his sword hilt growing slippery as blood slid down his arm.

She still has all the proof her father will need, he reminded himself. *She just needs to make it to him.*

Gavin launched himself at the guards once more. This time, the exchange of attacks was shorter, ending with his back pressed against the door and nowhere else to retreat to. *That's all I can manage.* His sword slipped from his grasp and fell to the floor as the remaining guards leveled their weapons at him. *Sorry, Tali.*

"Hold!"

Lord Kelmar had rounded the table, his hand close to his own sword hilt with an amused look in his eyes. "You are *not* the man I expected to see here, Sir Gavin."

"I could say the same thing," Gavin answered, keeping his eyes on the man he'd once trusted with Talianna's life. "Though, I wouldn't put it past you to have commandeered the rooms of the woman you tried to murder." He laughed at the duke's raised eyebrow and the surprise on the faces of the few other courtiers in the room—men he barely recognized, who seemed rather perturbed by the turn of events. "Yes, we know about that." He clamped his hand against the wound in his forearm as the guardsmen who'd defeated him grabbed his shoulders. "We know all of it. No matter what, your plans won't succeed." *I hope.*

Lord Kelmar's eyes flicked to the dead and wounded guardsmen on the floor. "I underestimated you both. I won't do that again." He took a sudden menacing step toward Gavin. "Where's the princess now?"

Gavin shook his head. "I have no idea. Ideally, she's getting as far away from you as possible." He couldn't help the contempt that came through his words. "You swore just like I did to protect the royal family, *on your honor.*"

Lord Kelmar's laugh came out more like a snort. "Honor? I gave that up years ago. All that matters in this age is power, and there's no power greater than the one that sits on the throne."

He drew himself up with a stern look at his allies—a general commanding his army. "Kennon, go secure His Majesty. If the princess shows up, do whatever you must to keep them apart." He leveled a stare colder than any of Talianna's royal looks at Gavin. "I'll be there after I deal with this…issue."

Sudden panic struck through Gavin's heart as the guards bound his wrists with what felt like knotted handkerchiefs. *I hope Talianna had enough time.*

"Find a bag to go over his head," Lord Kelmar ordered. "I don't want anyone recognizing him."

Even with the dire situation, Gavin couldn't deny a twitch of satisfaction as the men rushed to do their master's bidding. *At least one person doesn't assume all servants are invisible.* He gave the bonds around his wrists a cautious tug, wincing as the movement stung the cut running up his forearm. *I don't have much of a chance to escape from here. Out in the open, I might have more of an opportunity.*

"I'm surprised you survived the forest."

Gavin looked up in surprise as the duke spoke. Even with his suspicions, it was still shocking to hear the admission out loud. "You planned it?"

Lord Kelmar shook his head. "She was *supposed* to reach the fife unharmed; it wouldn't have been believable for her to mysteriously disappear in the woods. Some of my other compatriots took things into their own hands." Something like a thundercloud passed over the nobleman's face. "They've been dealt with." He crouched to pull Gavin's wrist knife from the body of a dead guardsman, examining the blade before tossing it across the room. "They didn't believe me when I told them it was a pointless endeavor anyway. I knew all along that you'd do whatever it took to ensure she survived the trip."

"I hold to my oaths," Gavin said from between clenched teeth. "Something you seem to have forgotten in your pursuit of power."

"Knights are all the same. Honor and duty, always." Lord Kelmar sighed as one of the guardsmen emerged from Talianna's bedchamber with a wide scarf. "It's a pity. I could've used a man like you." He gestured at the door with a curt order to the guards, "Get that over his eyes, and let's move."

Gavin closed his eyes as the blindfold went on, enveloping his head with soft blackness and distorting most sounds. The smell of lavender that normally clung to Talianna's clothes stirred his senses, and for a moment, he could picture her face silhouetted against the sunlit woods. He took a deep breath, the moment of peace broken as a firm hand wrapped around his bicep and shoved him forward.

Muffled sounds filtered through the blindfold as the guardsmen propelled him down the stairs and into what he guessed was the service corridor immediately below Talianna's rooms. While a few noises sounded like exclamations of dismay or consternation, he assumed that the presence of the duke—walking alongside the guards and their bound prisoner—was enough to deter most servants from voicing objection or confusion. *I can't believe I didn't see this in him before.*

After a few minutes of walking, a fresh breeze brushed across Gavin's skin. While he'd lost track of their direction, the warmth of sunlight on his clothes and the heady smell of flowers informed him that they'd made their way out of the palace and were somewhere on the grounds.

He dug in his heels unexpectedly, causing the guards to swear and one to lose his grip. The grasp on his upper arms renewed as

Gavin demanded, "Where are you taking me?"

"To do what the bandits failed to do," Lord Kelmar's voice said coldly somewhere ahead of him. "I knew I should've gotten rid of you as soon as His Majesty began pressuring his daughter to marry. The two of you were becoming too close for my comfort."

"You don't know anything," Gavin spat. "All you care about is removing anyone who might stand in your way."

Brilliant sunlight streamed into his face as the blindfold fell away. As his vision cleared, he realized where he was. Rose beds surrounded a fountain and carefully trimmed grass, the hedges beyond rising high enough to seclude the garden from sight. Arched gateways guarded each cardinal point, their white-painted lattices overgrown with climbing roses in vibrant pinks, yellows, and reds. He caught his breath with a gasp as the memories swept in—laughter and play, his world crashing apart on the heels of a single embrace, and the vision of a small girl with the world on her shoulders.

It's the garden.

Too late, he realized that Lord Kelmar had said something else. Gavin's knees hit the ground, the sun warming the back of his neck as metal cleared a sheath with a ringing sound. *Sorry, Talianna. At least we had a little time.*

Before any blow could land, another sound broke the tension. An offset rhythm of clanging bells sounded from the palace, the clamor growing and inciting a surge of adrenaline within his veins.

The guardsmen both tensed. "What the—?"

Gavin doubled over as a boot slammed into his stomach and the duke's voice built to a scream. "What have you done?!"

He coughed, caught his breath, and—laughed. "You underestimated us again, *Sir.* You thought I was a threat, but you didn't stop to think what Talianna might be capable of." He locked eyes with his former commander, fear swept away in the tide of bells and memories of children's laughter. "She's hidden behind her crown all these years, but you have *no idea* what kind of power you've been toying with. We didn't just know everything; we had proof, and you've given her time to get it into the hands of those you fear most. You're done for."

Lord Kelmar stepped back, fear mixing with growing anger in his face.

"Sir, you need to go!" one of the guardsmen urged.

"Not while he's still alive." A horrible sneer twisted Lord Kelmar's face, and his hand went to his own sword. The guardsmen's hands left Gavin's shoulders, and they took several steps away, fear almost palpable as their master advanced. "She may take the throne unhindered, but at least *you* won't be there to see it."

The ringing of the duke's sword being drawn echoed strangely through Gavin's mind, matched by dozens of others as a powerful voice resounded across the garden. "Stop!"

Lord Kelmar's head snapped around, and his eyes widened. In a heartbeat, he'd dropped his sword and was fleeing toward the opposite side of the garden, his men outpacing him as armed men poured through the archway that led to the palace.

Gavin blinked furiously; certain he was hallucinating as his second-in-command ran across the grass toward him with his sword drawn.

"Captain!" Tristan shouted. With a quick slash, the blood-soaked bindings holding Gavin's wrists fell away. Tristan pulled him to his feet, taking in his appearance with a whistle.

"Holy Lord of Light, man. She said you needed us, but I didn't realize how badly."

"—she?" Gavin whirled in the direction of the gate just as a tall, trim figure in a plain grey dress and bodice stepped through the archway. "Tali!"

In an instant, he was ten again; and this time, the princess wasn't walking away from him. He was never sure afterwards which of them was running faster, closing the distance toward each other at a pace that made all the years seem to fall away. They met in a skidding rush, Gavin catching Talianna around the waist and spinning to dispel their momentum. The world swirled, then settled, as he and Talianna clung to each other in a desperate, relieved embrace.

When he could finally think again, he asked, "How'd you find us?"

"I realized the duke would've heard from my uncle. He would've known we meant more to each other than our stations dictated, and I thought he might try to kill you." Talianna nodded to the gate on the far side of the garden, this one wrought-iron and barring the way to the wilder portions of the grounds. "I thought I saw that gate, but from the other side—the forest side. The trees, they said—I *saw* you." Her arms tightened. "You were on your knees. I don't know how to explain it, but I knew you were in danger." Her breathing quickened, and she looked up in terror. "We were almost too late! He was going to kill you!"

"But he didn't," he reminded her. "You saved me." A laugh built in his chest, pouring out all the relief and hope that words couldn't express. "You've saved me twice now." He glanced at the side of the garden. Curses and shouts drifted through the air as the men of Talianna's personal guard bound and dragged Lord

Kelmar and his men away. "It was close, too. I think I owe you a debt."

"No, that makes us even. Barely." She drew back from him and put her hands on her hips. "I don't care what protocol states, or what insanity you swore to. If I'm to be queen someday, that means I can release you. No more oaths."

Gavin pulled her back into his arms, the summer sun warm against his face as he kissed her deeply. "None," he whispered, running a finger down her tearstained face. "None, unless you count the ones we'll make to each other on our wedding day."

"Not that those are any better. Sickness, turmoil, poverty." Talianna gave a short laugh. "Maybe we should write our own."

He couldn't stop his smile. "I think you'll have enough trouble to contend with, once the court finds out that you've selected the younger son of a minor noble house as your intended."

She looked up at the castle with a set to her jaw—vibrant strength that had been locked behind the façade of royal perfection now released for the world to see. "Father will understand, and I don't care about the others. I know who I chose, and I chose the bravest, most stubborn, most sacrificial guardian the kingdom's ever known."

"Handsome, too," Gavin added with a laugh. He kept hold of her hand as they walked back through the rose garden, side by side.

"Handsome as well. And modest." The sunlight highlighted every speck of gold in Talianna's eyes as she stopped under the arch where, years ago, circumstances had torn them apart. She stood on her tiptoes to kiss him softly, the scent of roses and sunlight filling the air as she whispered, "I love you."

"I love you too."

13

BEYOND

As the chaos across the realm subsided, rumors spread. They spoke of foreign conspiracy, death and torment, a duke beheaded, and an earl's estate handed over to his stepson.

By the day of the princess's wedding, a whisper had made its way through the countryside and into the surrounding lands: *cross the royal family, and you'd fail.*

Why?

The gossips were never specific. Some muttered darkly of sorcery, others of old blood. Others—those with clear eyes and steadfast hearts—spoke of the unbreakable bond between the king, his daughter, and the guardian who'd given up his own safety to see theirs assured. Of such things were fairy stories made, yet hardly anyone knew how close to the truth the whispers trod.

The double doors swung open, allowing sunlight to stream into the hallway. Beyond the doors, the throne room was filled with people, their figures painted pink, green, blue and auburn in the puddles of light cast by the stained-glass windows.

Talianna took a deep breath, settling her shoulders as her

attendants processed down the carpet toward the archbishop with baskets of rose petals. Her veil brushed against her cheek as she glanced over her shoulder. "Do I look all right?"

A forest green tunic came into her periphery as Gavin stepped up to stand beside her. He gave her a smile with a twist of mischief. "You look terrible. We'd better call this whole thing off and get married in the stables."

"You're the worst," she accused, not even trying to hide her smile. "Thank you."

A flurry of trumpets sounded a fanfare. At the steward's nod, she and Gavin stepped forward, walking into the throne room side by side. The sunlight kissed her face through the veil as they stopped before the archbishop, and the wedding ceremony began. As she and Gavin turned to face each other, the thought occurred to Talianna how unlike this day was to the night he'd sworn his oath of protection.

It was dark, that night, she thought as they clasped hands. *We didn't know how each other had changed over the years apart, or what would happen from that day onward. Yet, even then, we both knew it was a moment that would carry us through the rest of our lives.*

Gavin's fingers wrapped around hers. His voice didn't waver as he delivered his vows, a triumphant look in his eyes as the final words thundered through the hushed room. As the priest turned to Talianna, surety settled in her stomach.

Forever seen. Forever protected. Forever loved, now and always.

She released Gavin's hands to reach up and brush the veil back from her face. A flicker of uncertainty ran in whispers through the congregation—this wasn't the point in the traditional ceremony for such a thing to occur. *I don't want a single barrier between us. Never again.*

"I, Princess Talianna, pledge to take this man as my wedded husband, in accordance with the faith and in the sight of these witnesses. From this day onward, I promise to love, honor, and guard him through sickness, storm, and turmoil, for as long as we live." The sunlight warmed her face, gently washing away the fears of lonely years. Talianna took a deep breath and looked straight into the eyes of the man who'd seen past the crown to the princess.

"So do I swear."

ACKNOWLEDGEMENTS

Let me tell you a story...

It's December, 2011. I'm freezing my behind off in a drafty chemistry lab. Class is twice a week, three hours long, and deathly boring. The professor grades on such a steep curve that I barely need to study, but I do have to attend for my grades to count. So here I sit, notes open with a composition notebook sitting atop them. Within those pages, over a semester of equations and falling asleep with my cheek in my hand, the story of a knight and princess comes into being.

Then I get married. I have children, piece my mind together after it breaks, and survive a pandemic as a hospital worker. The following year, I publish my first book and step into the world of indie publishing. I make friends, including Brittany Eden and AJ Skelly of Quill & Flame Publishers. A year later, Brittany comes to me with an offer. Publish an anthology with me, she says. We'd call it *Crowns*, theme it around royalty, and build into her existing fairytale series. And that fantasy romance novella I'd talked about? We'd publish it as the anchor.

In December of 2023, *Crowns* releases with *Guardian's Oath* as the featured novella. The princess hiding behind her crown and the knight sworn to defend her against all odds finally have readers who love them. And now, they stand on their own.

I've written a few more books since then, and this story feels like an outlier in that backlist. I mean, fantasy romance? Pink roses, sunlight through leaves, and kisses in a stairwell? What happened to the bloodshed, angst, and high stakes…oh wait.

It's obvious to me, now five years into this authoring thing, that *Guardian's Oath* isn't as much of an oddball as I first thought. We have a white knight hero (Gavin's sigil is a white falcon, for crying out loud), themes of being known and loved, a friends-to-lovers relationship, sacrifice, action, angst, and the overarching truth that you'll find home here.

Perhaps it's not that far from the mark after all.

As I wrap up and attempt to figure out my next steps in this world, thank you to the ones who've seen me this far. To Emmy and Laurel for the early critiques, Brittany and AJ for catapulting me into this world, Ava and the crew for a glorious cinematic trailer, Amber, Bryn, and Crystal for endorsing, and Robin for making this story a comfort reread. Thank you as well to the friends I've met while lost in the woods (if you think it might be you, you're correct). The light shines brighter in my life because it's reflected off you.

Finally, welcome to the ones who feel unseen. *Guardian's Oath* is for you.

ABOUT THE AUTHOR

Brigitte Cromey isn't certain how she ended up writing a bodyguard x princess romance, but stands by her decision to repeatedly make her characters' lives interesting. She writes stab-by books that feel like home from a lair in southern Arizona, where she shares life with her childhood best friend/husband of thirteen years and their small horde of barbarians. In what spare time she doesn't have, she can also be found learning new ethnic recipes, watching anime, and ~~ignoring~~ cultivating a handful of houseplants in an effort to make her home feel more like a forest and less like a cave. Despite her sharp-edged nature, she's a secret softie and will never let a story end without hope.

FURTHER READING

Tales of Sea & Skies
Star of Hope
Fires of Freedom

The Aftermath Trilogy
The Shattered Ones
In the Unbreaking
Hearts Invincible

Fates Defiant
(with C.M. Banschbach)

Crowns: A Heartbooks Anthology
(with Brittany Eden)

www.ingramcontent.com/pod-product-compliance
Lightning Source LLC
Chambersburg PA
CBHW020808310726

48969CB00002B/757